The Son of His

(Volume 3)

Mrs. Oliphant

Alpha Editions

This edition published in 2024

ISBN : 9789357968478

Design and Setting By
Alpha Editions
www.alphaedis.com
Email - info@alphaedis.com

Contents

CHAPTER I. THE GREAT SCHEME..............................- 1 -

CHAPTER II. MR. SANDFORD'S
SECRETARY. ....- 8 -

CHAPTER III. JOHN ON HIS TRIAL. ....- 15 -

CHAPTER IV. DEFEATED AND
WRONGED. ....- 22 -

CHAPTER V. THE CULPRIT. ....- 29 -

CHAPTER VI. A CRISIS....................................- 35 -

CHAPTER VII. MRS. SANDFORD'S
VIEW. ....- 41 -

CHAPTER VIII. THE CONVICT. ....- 48 -

CHAPTER IX. THE FIRST SHOCK. ....- 55 -

CHAPTER X. MOTHER AND SON. ....- 62 -

CHAPTER XI. SUSIE AND HER
LOVERS. ....- 70 -

CHAPTER XII. JOIIN'S LETTER. ....- 78 -

CHAPTER XIII. THE DARKNESS
THAT COULD BE FELT. ....- 86 -

CHAPTER XIV. THE VALLEY OF HUMILIATION.....................................- 93 -

CHAPTER XV. THE FATHER AND CHILDREN. ....- 102 -

CHAPTER XVI. THE GREAT SCHEME. ....- 109 -

CHAPTER XVII. ELLY'S PLEDGE.................................- 116 -

CHAPTER XVIII. A SUSPENDED SOLUTION..- 123 -

CHAPTER I.

THE GREAT SCHEME.

JOHN'S imagination, though it was so full of other matters, was affected more than he could understand by his strange visitor. He felt himself going back a hundred times in the course of the evening to this man, and those curious sophistries which he produced, always with that half smile in his eyes, as if he himself saw the absurdity in them, and as if morals and reason were something outside of himself to be treated with entire impartiality.

John wondered how far he believed or disbelieved what he had been saying, and whether these dispassionate discussions of what was formally right or wrong took away from a conscience, which could not be very delicate or sensitive, anything of the burden. They set him thinking too, following the career of such a being, trying to understand. Drink—was not in the decalogue, as his visitor had said: and John had seen enough even in his short life to know with what facility, with what innocence of evil meaning, the first step may be taken in that most general, most destructive of all vices—the one which leads to so many other developments, and which involves, as that philosopher had allowed, consequences more terrible, and penalties more prompt and inevitable than any other. John was very strenuous against it, almost bitter, having seen, as everyone has seen, its disastrous effects upon both body and soul. And yet, perhaps it was true what the other had said. Perhaps there were sins which brought no immediate evil consequences, which yet were blacker in the sight of heaven.

He felt himself wondering, with an indulgent feeling which was strange to him, how it was that a man who had nothing in him of the criminal air, a man full of thoughtfulness and humorous observation, and a knowledge of the workings of the mind, should have fallen into crime, and should have sunk into those depths and abysses of misery where he had no friend but Joe. A man must have reduced all the motives of human life to their elements, he must have banished all consideration of the outward and visible, all thoughts of the alleviations, the consolations, the comforts and stays of existence before he could have sunk contentedly to the bottom, and cynically, stoically, smilingly, despairingly, made himself believe that his brutal 'mate' was as good as any other, being all that remained to him.

And what, John asked himself, could remain for a convict whose world for so many years had been limited to the interior of a prison, and who in the course of working out his sentence had lost everything? What remained? One would suppose the poor wretch's family, somebody who belonged to him, some wife or sister, or daughter. And then came his story: It is Corban—a gift. John felt his own heart bleed at the mere thought of this hopeless, succourless, yet uncomplaining misery. A man who could manage still to smile in the face of all that, to maintain still the attitude of a thinker, of an observer looking on at his own entire destitution with impartial eyes, with that calm and full understanding and humorous despair—the young man shuddered in the midst of his own success and prosperity, and love and hope. Could there be a more complete and absolute contrast? It was so great that his heart seemed to stand still as he contemplated it—a distance as of heaven from hell.

The evening was spent in very close work; for he found that a great many details had to be filled in and made clear before the plan, worked out in his own brain, could be made presentable to the experienced and critical eyes to which he meant to submit it. And he was at his writing-table again early in the morning, arranging his papers so as to make the copying easy, with much question in his own mind whether his new *protégé* would really come, whether he would prove capable of such work. John thought that in all likelihood the man would not come, and was giving up with a regret which seemed even to himself quite uncalled for—regret as for a pet project which he gave up most unwillingly—the plan of active charity which he had so hastily adopted—when his visitor of the previous day suddenly appeared. He came alone, trim and well-brushed, but with a shaking hand, and eyes which were red and muddy, and made his excuses with a deprecating smile.

'I'm late,' he said, 'you must make allowance for bad habits. And I've had to get up as other people pleased for so long that I can't help indulging a little now; but I work quickly and I'll soon make it up.'

'There is no hurry,' said John: which was not exactly true, nor what he would have said to anyone else. And they worked together for the greater part of the day, not talking much, though John's secretary now and then paused, leaned back upon his chair, raised his eyes to the ceiling, and seemed on the eve of resuming the philosophisings of last night. But John was too busy to take any notice, and his companion presently would fall to work again.

He had no special knowledge of John's subject, but he had a great deal of intelligence, and asked reasonable questions and led John into explanations which were very useful to him, showing him how to recommend and elucidate his plan. They had their chop together in the middle of the day, and John found his companion more and more agreeable. There was something natural, familiar, in the relations into which they fell. John was a young man not too easy, as his fellow-workers knew, to 'get on with.' He was very exacting in the matter of attention to work. He was apt to conceive a contempt for the people who did not care for what they were employed on—and the young men who did just what they were compelled to do and no more, found no favour in his eyes. But even those periods of idling which occurred in the work of this grey-haired secretary did not produce that effect upon his young employer.

A gentleness of feeling, little habitual to him, stole over John. He did not feel critical—he felt friendly, oh, so compassionate, afraid even to think anything that could add a pang to this man, so forlorn and miserable, denuded of all things. The less he made of his own wretchedness the more profoundly did John feel it. He kept thinking, as he gave him his instructions, of all that this clear intelligence must have suffered shut up in the strait routine of a prison. He could not copy a page or make a calculation without some little running-over of remark, something that brought a smile, that betrayed the lively play of a mind unsubdued by the most tremendous burdens, by all the heavy and horrible experiences of such a life. How could he have borne that, day by day and year by year? A sort of awe, and almost reverence of the tragedy that this humorous, light-hearted being must have lived through, rose in John's musing soul.

It was not until they were finishing their little meal together that the absence of one very natural and usual explanation between them struck the young man.

'By-the-by,' John said, suddenly—he was making corrections in one of the papers and did not raise his head—'By-the-by, it seems very absurd. I don't even know your name.'

There was a moment's silence, and then John looked up. He found his companion's eyes fixed upon him with his usual half smile of observation, and dubious humorous uncertainty. When John met his eye he changed his position a little with a momentary laugh.

'I have been so long out of the habit of thinking a name necessary,' he said. 'My name is——' He paused again, and once more looked at John, in whose face there was no suspicious anxiety, but only a friendly alertness of interest. Something mischievous and mirthful lighted up in the stranger's eyes: 'My name is—March,' he said.

'And mine is Sandford,' replied John.

The mischievous light went out of the other's look. His face grew serious; he nodded his head two or three times with gravity.

'I know that,' he said. 'It is a name that I have had a great deal to do with in my life; but I don't suppose you ever heard of me.'

John shook his head. He cleared away with his own hand the last remnants of the luncheon, over which enough time had been expended.

'Now we'll get to work again if you are ready,' he said.

He knew nothing of any March. He was not aware that he had ever heard the name. And then they set to work again together pleasantly, cheerfully; John finding something inspiriting in the companionship for all the rest of the afternoon.

Next day the young man presented himself at the office, though his leave was not yet exhausted. But he did not go naturally to his own desk, to look if there were letters or special orders for him. He marched straight to the door within which the younger partner, the son of the Mr. Barrett who had received him into the office, and whom John had always found severe, had his throne. The younger Mr. Barrett was far more favourable to the young man than his father had ever been, and never spoke to him of the hospital, or the duty which lay upon him to repay his mother for her kindness, which was what the elder invariably did. It is not a subject which is agreeable even to the most dutiful of children. Repay your mother for all that she has done for you! Who could bear that odious advice? John was not angelic enough to be pleased by it. And when he had the choice it was to Mr. William Barrett that he betook himself. He found that personage in a very cheerful condition, and delighted to see him.

'You are the very man I want. You must go off at once to those works at Hampstead. They've got into a mess, and no one can clear it up better than you. I was just wishing for you. But your leave is not out: how is it you've come back before your time?'

Then John explained that he had been privately working for a long time at a scheme of which his mind was very full. And he gave on the spot an account of it which made the junior partner open his eyes.

'If you've done that, my boy, you've made your fortune, and ours too,' he said, listening with great attention to John's exposition.

'That's what I hope, sir,' the young man said, with all the confidence of youth.

Mr. William Barrett listened half-bantering, half-believing. To think of so young a man having hit upon an expedient which had baffled so many older brains, seemed to him half-incredible, and he laughed and rubbed his hands even while he seriously inclined to hear all the details of the scheme.

'It all depends upon whether it's practicable,' he said. 'Do you know the lie of the country? Have you calculated the cost even of what will be required as a basis of operations?'

'I have calculated everything,' said John, with that enthusiastic conviction which is so contagious. Mr. Barrett looked in his face with a laugh, half-sceptical, half-sympathetic.

'I like young men to think well of their own schemes,' he said; 'and I like them to plan big works even if they should never come to anything. Show me your papers——'

'I am having them copied out. I am making the statement as clear as possible. I will bring them as soon as they are ready.'

'Oh, they are not ready, then!' Mr. Barrett cooled perceptibly. 'You should not have said anything about it until they were in a state to be inspected—copying was not necessary—the rough notes are what I should have liked to see. You had better go off to Hampstead at once, and when you have finished that job you can bring me your plan, if it is ready then. There may be something in it—one can never tell.'

John felt that this was a very summary dismissal after the gleam of favour with which he had been regarded. He felt as if the plan which had been so much in the forefront of his imagination had been cast all at once into the background, which discouraged him for the moment: all the more that his own judgment agreed with what his chief said, and he felt now that it would have been better to place the scribbles of his rising invention before the experienced eyes which could see at a glance what was practicable in them, instead of the fair copy written out in a strange hand, which his impulse in favour of poor March had alone moved him to make. However, he set out at once for Hampstead, according to his orders, and there forgot his discouragement, and even, for a time, his great scheme, in the counter excitement of bringing order out of chaos. There is a certain satisfaction in finding that a piece of business has been horribly mismanaged, when one feels that one can put it all right. For some days John was fully occupied with this work, with scarcely time even to think of anything else. He got home at night late and very tired with his day's work, feeling able for little more than to give a glance at what March had been doing and to feel the comfort and satisfaction of having an amanuensis who arranged his papers so carefully and copied so neatly, in a handwriting, which, John remarked with surprise, was very like though better than his own. Everything was carefully arranged in the most orderly manner, the scraps of calculation in their proper succession, and the work going on, though slowly. It was indeed going on very slowly, and John never found his secretary at work when he returned: but he reflected that in all likelihood that philosopher, left to himself, took things easily; and there was no hurry: and he was too tired in the evenings when he came back from his work to give his full attention to anything else.

The Hampstead work occupied him for about a fortnight. On the morning after its completion he got up with a new start of energy, and with a revival of interest and enthusiasm betook himself to his great scheme. To his surprise, however, he found the little collection of calculations, sketches, and estimates, in the very same condition in which he had placed them in March's hand, all very neatly arranged and in proper order, but without a trace of the fair copy for which he had given instructions. John was exceedingly startled, and did not know what to think. Had it not been done at all? had the patience of the unfortunate amanuensis or his self-control given way, and the work been thrown up? But then John had seen a considerable part of it completed. He had even, as has been said, looked over a portion of it, and remarked that March's handwriting was like his own. What could this mean? An alarm which he felt to be absurd, at least excessive, most likely altogether uncalled-for, took possession of him. He called his landlady and asked her if Mr. March had said anything, if he had left any message, if he had been at work the day before? John's landlady was the impersonation of respectability: she did not lose her temper or break forth into abuse. But her air was that of an offended woman, and she immediately replied that she had been about to speak to him on the subject, that she could not have such persons in her house.

'Persons?' John said, with surprise, and then Mrs. Short, keeping her composure with difficulty, informed him that she had nothing to say against 'the old gentleman,' who she allowed was pleasant-spoken, and looked respectable, though she much feared he liked a drop: but that the other was the one as she could not abide.

John learned with some annoyance that Joe had come daily while he was absent, and had made his way into the room where March sat at work—but that for the last two days neither of them had appeared at all.

'And very glad I was: for I couldn't have stood it another day, not another day, Mr. Sandford, much as I think on you, sir. A fellow like that slouching in as if the place belonged to him: and who could tell what he mightn't bring—disease, or vermin, or dirt: dirt sure enough, for Jane did nothing but sweep up after him. Glad was I when they both went away.'

'The day before yesterday?' said John, 'and no message, not a word to explain.'

'The old gentleman came in the morning. He had the papers out as usual, and was a-going to begin: and then the other one came for him, and they both went away.'

All John's questions could elicit nothing more than this. He said to himself that March must have taken something to finish at home; that perhaps he might have fallen into one of those paroxysms of drinking with which John was acquainted among his men. He was angry with himself for the apprehensions that stole into his mind. If this man had not been what he was—a convict, a man without a character, John said to himself, it never would have occurred to him to fear. Joe, indeed, was not to be trusted with spoons or even great-coats or anything portable; but what could Joe know about the value of his papers? It was ridiculous to think of any theft. No doubt the easiest explanation was the true one—that March had taken the papers to complete at home. With this he tried to content himself, and, with the idea that after all he was but doing what he ought to have done at once, gathered up his own rough notes and calculations, and set out for the office. There seemed a slight excitement there at his appearance, or so he thought. The vague uneasiness in his own mind no doubt gave a certain aspect of curiosity and commotion to the clerks in the outer office, who looked up at him as he came in.

'Mr. Barrett, I think, was looking for you, Sandford. You will find them both in Mr. William's room,' said the principal of the outer office.

John walked in, not without a growing sense of trouble to come; he did not know what it might be, but he felt it in the air. Some thunder-bolt or other was about to fall upon his unaccustomed head.

CHAPTER II.

MR. SANDFORD'S SECRETARY.

THIS was what had happened in the meantime, while John had been about his other work. The man whom he had so readily taken up, knowing nothing of him except harm, had begun with quite an *élan* of sympathetic industry while the young man was with him. It was his nature so to do; had John remained with him all the time he would have continued so, with a generous desire to second and carry out all his wishes. But, when left alone to his work, his interest flagged. He settled everything in the most neat and orderly way, for he was always orderly, always ready to arrange and keep a certain symmetry in his surroundings, a kind of gratifying occupation which was not work.

When he had spread out his ink, his pens, his pencil, and ruler, his blotting-paper, and all the scraps he had to copy on the table before him, he began his work, and wrote on for half-an-hour at least with the air of a man who knew no better pleasure. But when he got to the conclusion of the page he laid down his pen and began to think. He had a quickly working mind, readily moved by any suggestion, taking up a cue and running on from it in lines of thought which amused him sometimes with a certain appearance of originality, enough to impose upon any chance listener, and always upon himself. This led him into mental amplifications of the text that was before him, and gave him a certain pleasure at first even in his work of copying. He thought of two or three things which he felt would be great improvements upon John's plan as he went on, and at the end of each page he mused for an hour or so upon that and a hundred other subjects into which it ran. And then he roused up suddenly and turned the leaf and wrote a few sentences more; and then it occurred to him that it was time to eat something, as his breakfast had been a very light one.

He went out accordingly, having still money in his pocket, to get his luncheon, and lingered a little to wash down the hot and savoury sausage which was agreeable to a stomach not in very good order, and met Joe, who was hanging about on the outlook for his mate. Joe returned with him to pilot his friend safely through the little-known streets to the room in which John, in his simplicity, had believed his protégé would be safe from all such influences, and went in with him to bear him company. Then, after March had rested from these fatigues, his comrade aroused his interest not unskilfully.

'I 'eard him say,' remarked Joe, 'as them papers would make 'is fortin.'

'So he thinks, poor lad; and I hope they may, for he's a good lad and has been very kind to me.'

'Droll to think you can make a fortin' by writin' on bits of paper,' said Joe, touching John's notes with his grimy hand (and indeed that opinion is shared by many people), 'is it story-books, or wot is it!'

Mr. March laughed with genuine enjoyment, leaning back in his chair.

'No, you ignoramus,' he said; 'don't you see its figures, calculations, things you can understand still less than story-books? It's a great scheme, Joe, my fine fellow, for turning the water out of the river and making the floods into dry land.'

'You're laughing at a poor fellow, guv'nor. I aint no scholard. And what'll be done with the land? Will he farm it, or build on't, or what'll he do with it, when he's got it? Doin' away with the river would be little good, as I can see.'

'Joe, you are a donkey,' said his mate; 'don't you know there's floods every year, and water in the houses, and water on the fields, and destruction everywhere. And this young fellow is an engineer, and means to put a stop to that.'

'Oh!' said Joe. Then, after a pause, he added, 'It 'ud be the landlords o' them places that would get the profit o' that.'

'Landlords and everybody; it would be a great advantage to the country, and would make our young man's fortune, as he says.'

'If I was you,' said Joe, 'I'd go on ahead with that. If it's you that's writing it out, you'll go shares in the profits, I reckon.'

March resumed his pen at this incentive and began once more to write.

'No,' he said, shaking his hand, 'not shares; for I have really nothing to do with it except to copy it; but I've no doubt he will pay me, and pretty well too——'

'I daresay,' said Joe, 'if he's that sort of a cove for finding out things, as he has a many more in his head as well as this.'

'I should think most likely,' said the elder man. 'He's got a good brain—and plenty of energy, and fond of his profession—which is a good thing, Joe. Neither you nor I have been fond of our professions, unfortunately for us.'

'I ain't got one—not even a trade. I was brought up to hang about, and do odd jobs. I never had no justice in my bringing-up.'

'Ah, that was a pity,' said his companion; 'perhaps, however, it wouldn't have mattered much. Hanging about is the trade of a great many men, Joe, more successful men than you and me.'

'It depends on the nature o' the jobs you gets,' Joe remarked. He drew his chair a little nearer to the writing-table. 'I'd get on with that there work, guv'nor, if I was you,' he said, with a nudge; 'if there's a fortune in it for one, there might be a fortune in it for two.'

March looked at him hazily with an afternoon look of drowsiness and languor; but he was tickled by the advice thus given, and resumed the so-easily-relinquished work. Joe, so to speak, sat or stood over him all day, encouraging and stimulating. The work went on slowly, as John remarked in the evening, but still it went on. The next day and the next passed in much the same way, except that Joe, 'hanging about' as usual, managed to meet his comrade on his way to instead of after luncheon, and so secured a clear head and less drowsy condition for the afternoon. At last, chiefly by the exertions of this very unusual overseer, the work was concluded, and then Joe spoke his mind more clearly.

'It's you as has had most part of this work, guv'nor, but it's he as'll get the pay.'

'That's the way of this world, Joe,' said his comrade. But he added after a moment, with a magnanimous air, 'Not in this case, however—for I have only copied, I have not invented—though I may have given a few hints.'

He had given these hints only to himself, various suggestions having occurred to him in the course of his copying, which in some instances he had inserted with the wildest ignorance of practicability in his text.

'I make no doubt,' said Joe, 'as the best of it come out o' your head, guv'nor. You was always the one as had the brains; and it's you as should profit by it. A young fellow like that's got no occasion to make his fortune at his age. It ain't good for him. When you make your fortune like that right off, it puffs you up with pride, and it stops you doing more. Ain't that true? Why, you knows it is;—chaplains and parsons and all that sort say so. It's good for you to be kep' down when you're young. It would be a thousand pities to spoil a young fellow's life like, with getting everything that he wants first thing afore he's had any experience. That's what has always been said to me.'

'There is some truth in it, no doubt,' said March.

'A deal of truth, guv'nor. I suppose, now, you've just got to take them papers to somebody as deals in things like that, and get money for 'em down on the nail?'

'He will take them to some great engineering firm,' said the other. 'And probably he would not part with them for a sum "down on the nail," as you say. Such a scheme as this he'd be sure to have some share in it. He would superintend the carrying out of his plans, if you understand that. It might be years of work for him, and the most excellent beginning. I should think he deserved it, too,' said John's amanuensis, looking round approvingly, 'for there is every evidence that he's a fine fellow, and I know he has been very kind to me.'

'And you might be very kind to 'im, in that way,' said Joe.

'I could be—kind to *him*? I don't think I've very much in my power one way or other,' said March, with a smile and a sigh.

'Guv'nor,' said Joe, 'you never was one as took things upon you. Give up to other folks, that was allays what you would do. But what's the good? You don't get no thanks for it. If I was in your place—as I'm a donkey, and good for nothing, but you ain't, and could do a lot if you liked—I know what I'd do.'

March smiled benignantly enough upon the poor dependent, whose flatteries were not unpleasant to him.

'And what would you do, if you were me, which is not a very likely change?' he said.

'No, it ain't likely. Them as is born asses, dies asses—and t'other way too. It ain't for me to tell a clever man like you, and that has got a fine education, and born a gentleman.'

'Alas!' said March, shaking his head; 'alas! it hasn't come to much, has it? Your mate, my poor fellow, and one without a friend but you, or a chance in the wide world——'

'Don't say that, guv'nor. Here's a chance, if I ain't more of a born ass than ever I thought—a chance for a fortune, and for doing the young fellow a good turn. How's he, at his age, to show up a big thing like this? There's nobody as would believe it of him. They'd say, "Oh, get along, you boy." They'd never take him in earnest at all.'

'I do him a good turn! I, a broken man, without character or anything; without a friend! and he a fine, respectable young fellow, well thought of, and clever, and knowing more than I ever knew at my best. That's nonsense, Joe.'

'Not if you'll think a bit, guv'nor; I hear him say them papers is my fortune—and then I hears him 'eave a sigh. He's not one of the pushing ones, he isn't. He knows as they're worth a deal, but he hasn't the face to say "Look here, you give me so much for this." Guv'nor, I know you're a man as will do a deal for a friend. Why don't you take 'em just as they lies there, and take 'em to some person as deals in that sort of thing, and just up and ask 'em what'll they give for this? "There's a young un," says you, "as understands everything about it and is just the man to work 'em out." If I were in your place, guv'nor, that's what I would do.'

'But, my good fellow,' said March, 'those papers belong to the young man here, not to me.'

'Guv'nor,' said Joe, 'I don't doubt as the best that's in that long story as you're writing out there comes out o' your own 'ead. It stands to reason as you know more about it than a young feller like 'im.'

The philosophical gull, who never learned wisdom, was touched by this in the most assailable point.

'It's true,' he said, 'Joe,—though how you've found it out I can't tell—that I have carried out a suggestion or two, and put in something that seemed to me the logical consequence of what he said. But nothing practical, for I don't understand the practical part. And how does that sort of thing give me any real claim?'

'Guv'nor,' repeated Joe, 'you needn't tell me. I know you, and how you're always giving up to other folks. It's half yours and more, I'll be bound. And the best you could do for the young 'un is just what I tells you. I'm practical, I am. If it was anything in my way, I'd do it like a shot; but it ain't in my way. The outsides o' things has a deal of power in this world. You in your fine respectable suit, you can go where you please like a prince. But me, it's "Be off with you—get along with you;" they won't say nothing of that sort to you. And you'll just make the young man's fortune, that's what you'll do. Say as he's the very one to look after the works and knows all the practical part. They ought to settle something handsome on you at once as your share and take him on as foreman, or whatever it is; and in that way you'd both get the best of it and all done well.'

The convict philosopher shook his head. He rose up from the table and put the papers away. He admired the neatness of his own manuscript extremely, and he was of opinion that he had done John a great deal of good by the suggestions which he had worked out and the additions which he had made. It was possible that Joe might be right, and that the best thing he could do for his young employer was what the poor faithful fellow had suggested. He had himself a great admiration, after having been deprived of it so long, of his respectable suit and appearance, and there was a great deal of plausibility, he thought, in what the man said. But it was still clear to him that John might not think so. He was not very rigid himself upon any point of morals, after his long practice in thinking everything over, and blurring out to his own satisfaction the lines of demarcation between right and wrong; but he could understand that the young man, not having his experience, might think otherwise; and he had even a sympathy for his want of philosophical power in that respect. So he put everything aside very tidily, and put his hand upon Joe's arm and drew him away, shaking his head, but not angry at the good fellow's insistence. There was something in it—and it might doubtless be under certain circumstances the most kind thing that could be done for the young man. Still there was the difficulty that the young man might not see it in that light. And Mr. March accordingly put up the papers, and taking Joe by the arm, with a benevolent smile and a shake of the head, led him away.

It has been said that John's rooms were in Westminster, not far from Great George Street, where the offices of Messrs. Barrett were, and where, as the reader needs not to be informed, various other engineers' offices are to be seen. March's eye caught the names involuntarily as he passed by. It was not that he was trifling with temptation, for he did not consider Joe's suggestion as temptation. He was only turning over the possibilities in his mind, and merely as a matter of amusement, an exercise of fancy, just as he might have counted how many white horses passed in the street, or which windows were curtained and which not, he read over to himself the names on the doors. Messrs. Barrett's was one which he weighed but afterwards rejected, as not liking the sound of it. Another quite near had a name that pleased him better—Messrs. Spender and Diggs. What a ludicrous combination! He laughed to himself at it, as it caught his eye. Spender and Diggs—it was highly suggestive, which was a thing dear to his mind at ease. It clung to his memory. He turned it round the other way to see how it would sound. Diggs and Spender: that was still more absurd.

And all the time Joe's voice was running on with arguments, the form of which, simple and subtle and couched in that language of the rough which is always more or less picturesque, amused his companion much. Joe had penetrated sufficiently into the mind of his mate to know how to address him. And that mind began to work upon the matter, with the amusing addition of the name of Spender and Diggs thrown in, and a great deal of pleasurable occupation in a question entirely characteristic and full of the difficulties he loved.

The result was that March appeared in the morning as the landlady had said, and spent a short time, but only a very short time in John's sitting-room. The copy was completed, carefully folded up, and put in a large envelope. All John's notes, the originals, were scrupulously left in their place, and in perfect order. For in some points his conscience was of scrupulous nicety, and John's notes were certainly his own and not to be tampered with. As he was going out with the large envelope in his breast pocket, John's landlady appeared with the remonstrance which had been on her lips for some days.

'You, sir, I've got no objections—a gentleman that's pleasant spoken and respectable even if he ain't my lodger, but only a friend, that's a different thing:—— but your—— that man——'

'My servant?' said March, with a quick sense of the comicality of the situation.

'Well, sir,' said the woman, with hesitation; 'I wouldn't keep on a man like that in my service if I was you.'

'He is not as bad as he seems,' the philosopher said, with a twinkle in his eye, 'but I foresaw your objections, and you shall never see him more.'

'If that's so, of course, there isn't another word to be said.'

'That's so; you may calculate upon it as a certainty,' the pleasant spoken gentleman said; and with a wave of his hand and a chuckle of enjoyment he went away.

The events thus described will explain the scene which John to his consternation and amazement encountered when he stepped into Mr. William's room at the office, and found himself confronted by both members of the firm.

CHAPTER III.

JOHN ON HIS TRIAL.

BOTH the partners were together in Mr. William's room. They had been having some sort of a consultation, it was evident, and both looked very grave. When John walked in at his ease, though a little anxious, they both turned round upon him with very serious faces—the younger man with a grieved air, the elder one rigid and solemn, like a judge before whom a criminal has appeared, whose conviction has been pre-accomplished, and who has come up for judgment. Mr. William Barrett had the air of hoping that some more evidence might be discovered which would possibly exonerate the accused, but his father's face showed no such hope. On the contrary, something of the 'I always knew how it would be' was in his look, as he turned sharply round at the opening of the door.

John was greatly surprised: but still more indignant at this reception of him. He walked up to the table at which Mr. Barrett sat. Mr. William stood with his back to the dusty fireplace close by. Neither of them spoke, but looked at him with that overwhelming effect of silent observation which makes the steadiest footstep falter, and conveys embarrassment and awkwardness into the most self-controlled being. John said 'Good-morning,' and they both acknowledged it: Mr. William by an abrupt nod, his father by the most solemn inclination of his head. The young man did not know what to say. He stood and looked at them, wondering, indignant, taking his little packet of papers out of his pocket. What had he done to be so regarded?—or had he perhaps come into the midst of some consultation about other matters with which they were pre-occupied? He said,

'Is there anything the matter?' at last, saying to himself that it was impossible he could be the cause of such concentrated solemnity, and looking at the younger partner with a half smile.

'There is a great deal the matter,' said Mr. Barrett.

'Yes,' said his son; 'it's rather a grave business, Sandford. I don't see it in quite the same light as my father. Still, it's at least a great want of confidence, a strange slur upon us, who, so far as I know, have nothing to reproach ourselves with in respect to you.'

'Certainly not, sir,' said John: 'you have always been very kind and given me every opportunity; but I hope on my part I have not done anything to make you suppose I am ungrateful, or have not appreciated my advantages.'

'We have nothing to complain of so far as the works are concerned. I think, sir, I may say that?'

'It is a point on which I should not like to commit myself,' said the senior partner. 'These works at Hampstead, so far as I hear——'

'They went wrong when he was away. He can't be blamed for that: he came back before his time and went over at once, and made every thing shipshape again. He can't be blamed for that. Whatever went wrong was after his leave began.'

'An engineer,' said the elder gentleman, in his rigid way, 'who means to do justice to his profession, doesn't want leave. The works are his first interest—he has no occasion to go away to amuse himself.'

'Oh, come, father! you're making that a fault which is no fault—and we have a ground of offence which is real enough. Sandford, you came here the other day and told me of a scheme you had for draining the Thames valley. You may say I was disposed to pooh-pooh it a bit; but I didn't say more than one does naturally with a young fellow's first ideas, which are always so magnificent. Do you think there was a reason in anything I said for transferring the papers as you've done to another firm?'

'I transfer them to another firm?' cried John, 'you must be dreaming. I have them here.'

'You have them there? Then what do Spender and Diggs mean by spreading it abroad that they have had such a scheme sent to them by one of the pupils in our office, but which we had not enterprise to take up?'

'Spender and Diggs!' John was so well acquainted with the name of the rival firm that it raised no sense of humour in his mind: but something quite different, that sense of rivalry which is so strong between the pupils and partisans of different schools. He made a little pause, staring at his younger employer. And then he said, 'I don't know the least in the world what you mean.'

'There is no ambiguity at all about my meaning. I say that Spender and Diggs are putting it about everywhere that a great scheme, worked out by one of our pupils, for the draining of the Thames valley, has been offered to them.'

John's countenance grew pale with horror and dismay. He cried out, sharply,

'Good heavens! Why, it cannot be Horrocks or Green?'

'Don't add slander to your other sins,' said Mr. Barrett, severely, 'or endeavour to take away the character of young men who are quite incapable——'

'So they are,' said John, in all good faith, 'quite incapable. That is true, sir; but I could not help thinking for a moment that I might have left some of my papers about, and that they might have picked them up—but you're right, sir; they couldn't do it—that is a great relief to my mind.'

The young man was so undisguisedly relieved and so perfectly straightforward in the whole matter, that William Barrett began to doubt. He cast a glance at his father, who, however, sat rigid and showed no relenting.

'Sandford,' said the younger man, 'you seem to speak very fair; but there's this fact against you—no one supposed it was anyone's scheme but yours; you are the only man in our office capable of anything of the sort; we all know that. And it's no crime; but it is a horrid thing all the same—a caddish, currish sort of thing—to abandon the people who have trained you and done you every justice, and carry what I have no doubt you believe would be profitable work to another house.'

'I—carry work to another house! It is quite impossible that you should believe that of me. I might have thought it if you had said I had killed somebody,' said John, with a faint smile of ridicule, 'for that's a thing that might be done in a moment's passion—but carry work to another house! You cannot believe that of me.'

'What has believing to do with it,' said Mr. Barrett, 'when there are the facts that can be proved? Don't lose time bandying words, Will. Sandford must see that after this there can be no further connection between us. He knows, of course, that his place at Spender and Diggs' is safe enough. Let him have what is owing to him and let him go. I took him without premium for his mother's sake, and for the same reason—for Mrs. Sandford is a very worthy woman—I've given him every advantage, although I expected something of this sort all along.'

'Why should something of this sort have been expected from me? What have I done? I have done no wrong—I have all my papers in my pocket. You said you would rather have the rough notes. Here they are, every one,' cried John, taking out the papers from the envelope and throwing them down on the table; 'here are all the calculations, diagrams, and drawings, and all. And now, Mr. Barrett, there is the question to settle which you've just mentioned, which you raised long ago,' said the young man, with a flush of pride and anger. 'That wretched premium! It shall be paid before the banks close to-day. That, at all events, I can settle at once.

You have flung it in my teeth more than once when I was powerless. Now I have it in my own hands. Your premium, of which you have thought so much, shall be paid to-day.'

'Stop there, Sandford,' said the younger partner. 'Father, I beg don't say anything more—let us understand the more important matter first. You say you have brought us all your papers here. And yet I am informed from Spender and Diggs that they have your scheme, all carefully written out and elaborated——'

'Ah!' cried John, with a keen and quick sensation as if he had been startled and could not draw his breath.

'Of course the information doesn't come direct from them. They wouldn't be likely to do anything so friendly. Prince heard all about it from one of their men. We can have him in, and you can ask him any questions you like. Even if I hadn't known by what you told me, I should have felt sure it was you who had done it,' said William Barrett, secure in his own command of the situation. Then he added to the man who answered his bell, 'Ask Mr. Prince to step this way.'

Mr. Prince had stepped that way; he had walked up to Mr. Barrett's table, in his precise little manner, smiling ingratiatingly when he met his master's eye, and had told his story before John said anything more. He stood a little behind Prince, so startled that he could scarcely understand what was being said, though he heard it all—recalling his recollections and making it plain to himself what had happened. He had not been in the habit of doing rash things, nor was he one who gave his confidence and trust easily; but as he stood in the office, hearing the clerk's glib story—and feeling himself like the spectator of the strangest little scene on the stage, instead of standing, so to speak, on his trial, and listening to the evidence of the principal witness against him—a rush of suggestions was going through John's head.

The extraordinary fact which never had seemed at all strange to him before, that he had taken into his house and into his confidence a man of whom he knew nothing, except that he was a returned convict, showed itself all at once to him in the clearest light. Even in his suddenly awakened consciousness of what had happened, he felt that to call the man whom he had thus trusted a returned convict, hurt himself as if it had been a stab. It was on this ground he had made acquaintance with him, because he was a man who had been punished for crime, and might fall into crime again if he were not bolstered up by friendly help and saved from temptation. This was what John had attempted to do, and, lo, here was the result. He came gradually to himself through the hot and painful confusion of this critical moment, and put a few questions to the clerk which left no doubt on the subject. When Mr. Prince's examination was over, William Barrett turned to the young man, his natural good nature and friendliness modified by the triumph of having gained a complete victory.

'Sandford,' he said, 'I don't pretend to understand your conduct one way or another. You came back from your holiday before your time, to tell me of this scheme of yours. I neither said nor did anything to discourage you, more than one does naturally to a young man. You were engaged in our work, and bred up in our office: that should have been reason enough against going to any other firm.'

'It is a thing which never entered into my mind.'

'But it did into your actions, apparently,' said the junior partner, with a not unnatural sneer.

'It is what I have expected all along,' said Mr. Barrett, piously folding his hands. 'It is what his mother expected, an excellent, much-tried woman, for whose sake——'

'Prince, you may go,' said William Barrett, 'and, for heaven's sake, father, stick to the question. Don't bring in other things which have nothing to do with it.'

John had a great struggle with himself. The foregone conclusion against him with which he had so often been confronted was the one thing which overcame his good sense and self-control. Ever since his grandfather's death it had been intolerable to him, and it was all he could do to suppress the boiling-over of passionate resistance to this systematic injustice; but with a great effort he restrained himself. He stopped the departing witness with a wave of his hand.

'Let Prince stay,' he said, in a choked voice. 'I think I perceive how all this has occurred. Look here, did your informant say who took the papers to Spender and Diggs? Did he say it was I?'

'I don't know,' said Prince, 'that he knew you.'

'I have not the least doubt that you asked him who it was. If he did not know me, he must at least have known something about me. Did he say it was I?'

'Well,' said the witness, somewhat unwillingly, 'he didn't know who it was. He said he thought it was an elderly man: but there are many people always coming and going about the office, and he couldn't be sure.'

'Do you think it likely,' said John, 'that I could have gone to Spender and Diggs' office without being recognised?'

'Sandford, this is all quite unnecessary,' said William Barrett. 'I did not accuse you of going to Spender and Diggs' office. You might have employed any agent; such a thing is not necessarily—indeed, it's not at all likely to be done by the principal himself.'

'Then this is what I'm accused of,' said John. 'I came and told you of my scheme, for as much as it's worth. You did discourage me, Mr. William, but good naturedly, telling me to go to Hampstead in the first place. I obeyed you, and finished that work last night. This morning I come to you with my papers in my pocket, ready to submit them to you according to your own instructions; and I am met with accusations like a criminal. Is it likely that between hands I should have gone to Spender and Diggs? Why should I come here now with my original papers if I had in the meanwhile sent a copy elsewhere? Do Spender and Diggs say they refused them? What are they supposed to have said? Why am I supposed to have come, the first moment I was free, back here———?'

'Were you told they were refused?'

'No, sir,' said Prince. 'On the contrary, they were taken into consideration, and thought to have something in them. That was what was reported to me.'

'Why, then,' said John, 'should I come back here?'

There was a momentary pause; and then William Barrett broke forth again.

'What's the use of talking of motives and reasons and why you did it? Evidently you did do it, and there's an end of the matter.'

'And of our connection,' said his father. 'A young man that's so false to his employers can have no more to do in our works or our office.'

'As you please, sir,' said John. He had made a pause of indignation, staring at his accusers, dumb with the passion of a thousand things he had to say—but what was the use? He shut his lips close, growing crimson with the strong effort of self-restraint. 'I am sorry this should be the end,' he said, controlling himself desperately, 'but, of course, if that is your opinion, I have nothing to say. Good-bye, sir,' the young man cried, unable to keep back that Parthian arrow, 'it must be a pleasure to you that I have justified your certainty, and gone to the bad at the end.'

'Sandford!' said William Barrett, as John hurried out; but the young man was too much excited to pay any attention. The junior partner followed him to the door of the office calling after him, 'Sandford—I say Sandford—Sandford!'

But John paid no attention. He rushed downstairs two or three steps at a time, and over the threshold which he had crossed so often with the familiarity of every day life. His feet spurned it now. He seemed to be shaking the dust from him as the rejected messengers were to do in the Gospel. No better servant had ever been, no more dutiful pupil, and he was conscious of this. He had never been without a thought indeed of advancement in his own person, of carrying out a work of his own: but all his knowledge, the knowledge acquired out of their limits in the privacy of his own self-denying and studious youth, had been at the service of his masters and teachers unreservedly at all times. He had never thought of sparing himself, of doing as little as was possible, which was the way of many of his fellow-pupils. He had done always as much as was in him, freely and with devotion. And as the climax of so many faithful years, he had brought to them this first fruits of his maturing thought, this plan so long cogitated, which had been to him what a poem is to a poet—the work in which all his faculties, not only of calculation and practical reason, but of thought and imagination had been concentrated. It was to be the climax, and now it was the end. Instead of sharing his honours with them and bringing them substantial profit, as he intended, he was sent forth with shame as a traitor, a false servant, a disloyal man. John's heart burned within him as, holding his head high, and spurning the very ground, he marched out of that familiar place.

The sting of injustice was sharp in his soul. He said to himself that he would offer no further defence, that he would not attempt to prove the deception that had been put upon him, or how it was that he had been robbed at once of his scheme and honour. If it could be believed for a moment by people who had known him for years that he was so guilty, he would make no attempt to explain. If ever an accusation was unlikely, unreasonable, inconsistent with every law, it was this.

CHAPTER IV.

DEFEATED AND WRONGED.

HE had walked a long way before he came to himself out of those whirling circles of thought in which the mind gets involved when it is suddenly stung by a great wrong, or startled by a poignant incident. With this strong pressure upon him, he had gone right away into the Strand, and along that busy line of streets into the din and crowds of the city, feeling, like a deaf man, that the noise around made it more possible to hear the voice of his own thoughts, and to endure the clangour of his heart beating in his ears. He walked fast, not turning to the right nor to the left, straight through the bewildering throng in which every man had his own little world of incident, of sentiment, and feeling undisturbed by the contact of others on every side.

At first it had been the keen tooth of that wrong, the undeserved disgrace that had fallen upon him, which had occupied all his sensations. But by degrees other thoughts came in. He had left Edgeley in haste to strike his blow for fortune and reputation, though he was so young, to qualify himself for a new phase of life, to put himself nearer at least to the level of Elly, to justify his own pretensions to her. The scene in Mrs. Egerton's room suddenly flashed before him as he walked, adding another and yet sharper blow to that which he had already received. He had said that he would succeed, that he should be rich, that he had the ball at his foot. This morning when he came out of his lodgings he had felt the ball at his foot. How could it be otherwise? He knew the value of his own work. It was a work much wanted, upon which the comfort of a district, the value of the property in it, and the lives of its inhabitants might depend. And he felt convinced that he had hit upon the right way of remedying this fault of nature which had given so much trouble and cost so much suffering. What hours and hours he had thought of it and turned it over! What quires of paper he had covered with his calculations! It did not perhaps seem romantic work; but all the poetry in John's nature had gone into it. It had been Elly's work, too, though Elly could not have done one of all those endless mathematical exercises. It had occupied his mind for two at least of those early lovely years in which imagination is so sweet: and his imaginations had been sweet, though they had to do, you would have said, with things not lovely, cuttings and embankments, and drawings, and figures upon figures, armies of them, calculations without end. His very walks and the exercise he took, the boating which was his favourite recreation when he had any time, had all been inspired and accompanied by this. While he waited outside a lock, he was busy calculating its fall, and the weight and force of the water, and studying the banks high or low, for his purpose. He had grown learned in the formations of the district, in its geology and its productions with the same motive. He had marked unconsciously where wood could be got at and bricks made for the future works, and when his eye travelled over the river flats to the line of cottages with dull lines upon their lower storey, showing the flood-mark to which the water had risen, there rose in him a fine fervour as he thought that by-and-by all such dangers should come to an end. Thoughts frivolous and unworthy, the light and trifling mental dissipations that beguile young minds, and the insidious curiosities and temptations with which they play, were all crowded out by these imaginations, which were so practical, so professional, so enthusiastic, so full of the poetry of reality. This was the way in which many months had been occupied. And now——!

It was a long time before John had sufficiently calmed himself down, and got the mastery of those whirling circles of ever-recurring thought which almost maddened him at first, to face the situation as it now stood. At first, and for a long time, it appeared to him that ruin as complete as it was undeserved had overwhelmed him; his good fame seemed to be gone, and the bitterness of the thought that people who knew him, and knew him so well, and who had years of experience of his integrity and faithful service, should have at once believed him guilty of such treachery, seemed to drown him in a hopeless flood; for how should he convince strangers of his honour if they had no faith in it? or how attempt to clear himself professionally when two of the chief authorities in his profession believed him to have behaved so? Would it be the best way, the only way, to shake the dust from off his feet and rush away to the end of the world where a man could work, if it were the roughest navvy work, and be free from false accusation and the horror of seeing himself falsely condemned. But, then, Elly! John plunged again deeper than ever into that blackness of darkness. He had boasted in his self-confidence of the success which was awaiting him, of the certainty of his prospects. He remembered now how Mrs. Egerton had shaken her head. And now here he stood with his success turned into failure, his confidence into despair; the people who knew him best refusing to hear him. He had no fear that Elly would refuse to hear him; but who else would believe? They would not, indeed, believe that he had been treacherous, or played a villain's part, as the Barretts did; but they would think that he had mistaken his own powers, that he was not what he imagined, that his account of himself was a boy's brag, and not a sober estimate of what he knew he could do. And how convince them, how remedy the evil? Was it possible that any remedy would ever be found?

He had gained a little calm when he began to ask himself this question. Out of the whirl of painful thoughts and passionate entanglement of all the perplexities round him, he suddenly came to a clear spot from which he could look behind and after. He found himself on the bridge crossing the river, having got there he scarcely knew how, coming back in the direction of the office and of his lodgings after a feverish round through all the noise of London. As he walked across the bridge, there suddenly came to him a recollection of his first beginning—how he had paused there with the letter in his hand with which he had been sent to the Messrs. Barrett by his mother. He had paused, angry and wounded and sore, and looked down upon the outward-bound ships, and for a moment had thought of forsaking this cold, unkindly world in which he had no longer any home or anyone who loved him, of tossing the letter into the river and going his own way, and taking upon himself the responsibility of his own life. He had not carried out that wild resolution. He had swallowed all his repugnances, his pride, his rebellious feelings, and accepted the more dutiful way: and till now he had never repented that decision. He paused again, and before him lay the same great stream leading out into the unknown, the same ships ready to carry him thither, into a world all strange, where nobody would know John Sandford had ever been accused of falsehood. The repetition of this scene and suggestion gave him a certain shock, and brought him back sharply to himself. John Sandford, John May—he had not then been sure which he was—his heart had risen against the woman who was his mother, who had distrusted him and taken from him his father's name. Now he was more or less ashamed of the boyish rashness which had set him against her decision in this respect. He was John Sandford now, beyond any question. What if, perhaps, this fever of indignation and despair which was in his veins might die down and pass away, as the other had done?

This brought him back to more particular questions. He had felt no doubt from the first moment as to what had really happened: that the man whom he had so foolishly trusted, whom he had no reason to trust, had played him false, and carried off the copy which John had given him to do, out of what had appeared to him pure benevolence, Christian charity—to the rival firm. That was perfectly clear to him, though in his indignation and fury he would not pause to explain. If it was explained ever so, it would not restore the scheme thus betrayed to its original importance, or place it, as he had intended, in all its novelty and originality and ingeniousness, in the hands best able to carry it out. In any case, his secret was broken, his ideas exposed to curious and eager competitors who might, and probably would, take instant advantage of them. John still felt that he was ruined, however it might turn out. And yet he might clear his honour at least, and show how he had been himself betrayed. He had begun to acknowledge this possibility, to breathe more freely, to feel the fumes of passion dispersing, and the real landscape, chilled and grey with all the rosy illusions of hope disappearing, yet still real and solid under his feet, once more coming into his sight, when he became suddenly aware of an approaching figure, very unwelcome, most undesirable to meet at such a moment, yet not to be ignored. Why should he turn up precisely now, that chance acquaintance to whom John had committed himself in the impatience of his boyhood, and with whom he had a sort of irregular, fictitious intercourse, more congenial to Montressor's profession and ways than to his own? It brought a sort of ludicrous element into his trouble to meet this man, to whom he was not himself but another, a being who had never existed save for that one night on which he had enacted a sort of little single-scene tragic-comedy as John May. Montressor was not a person to be eluded: he came forward with his hands stretched out, his shiny hat bearing down over the heads of the other passengers upon John, as if it had been a flag carried aloft, with the directest and straightest impulse.

'Me dear young friend,' he said, 'me brave boy! how glad I am to see ye.'

Montressor was a little better dressed than usual. The shiny hat was new, or almost new, though it had somehow caught the characteristics of the old one. His coat was good, his well-brushed aspect no longer giving so distinct an accentuation to his shabbiness. He put his arm within John's in the fervour of having much to say.

'Fate's been good to me,' he said, 'and when it's so in great things 'tis also in small. Here have I been watching for ye, wondering would ye pass hereabouts, to tell ye, me young friend, that once again good luck has come Montressor's way.'

'I'm glad to hear it,' said John; but what he felt was only a sort of dull half pang additional, a sense that good luck might now come in anyone's way save his, which was closed to it for evermore.

'That I'm sure of,' said the actor, 'it isn't very much we've seen of ye, John May, and I don't even know where to find ye. To tell the truth, in me shabbiness and me poverty I didn't care to know: for meeting you in the street is one thing and pursuing you to your lodging is another. No. Montressor was not one to shame his friends, even though 'twas virtuous poverty. But rejoice with me, me young friend—that phase is over, never, I hope, to come me way again.'

'Have you got an engagement?' asked John, wondering and reflecting upon the shabbiness which was as pronounced as ever one short week before.

'Better than that,' said the actor. He put his hand to his eyes with a mixture of fiction yet reality. 'Me eyes are full and so's my heart. Pardon me, young man. Once you saved her life—never knowing that small thing was the future Rachel, the future Siddons. Me dear friend! it is Edie that has an engagement. Edie, me chyild!'

'Edie!' cried John, and then he laughed aloud at the thought. Edie, that baby, to whom he had sent something the other day to buy a doll.

'Indeed, 'tis Edie, no one else. Ye haven't seen her for a great while. Ye don't know that she's sixteen or near it, and a genius. She has a right to it, sir. It's hers by inheritance. *My* chyild, and her mother's—who under the name of Ada Somerset took leading parts for years—I don't grudge it to her, me dear May. She has had devoted care. She has had a training, me dear sir, that began in her cradle—and now!' He laid his hand upon the heart that no doubt was as full of real emotion as if he had not had a word to say on the subject. 'And she is a good girl, and the ball at her foot,' he added, in a tremulous tone, with water standing in his eyes.

'The ball at her foot,' said John, with a harsh laugh. 'So had I yesterday—or, at least, so I thought.'

'There's something happened to you, me brave boy?'

'Nothing's happened: at least, nothing that's wonderful or out of the way. I'm supposed to have broken trust and disgraced myself. It's like the things that happen in your stage plays. I'm condemned for something I never thought of, and robbed by one to whom I tried to be kind. Go home and take care of Edie. Never let her try to be kind to anyone,' John said, 'it's fatal; it's nothing less than ruin.'

'Me dear boy, open your mind to me, and relieve it of that perilous stuff. It is the best way. Come, tell me. Montressor has but little in his power even now, but what he can do is always at his friends' disposal; and, if there's a villain to be hunted down, trust me, me brave boy—I'll hunt him to the death!'

'Why should I trouble you with my vexations?' cried John. But in the end he yielded to the natural satisfaction of recounting all that had happened to a sympathetic—almost too sympathetic—ear. Montressor's was no indifferent backing of his friend. He threw himself with his whole soul into the wrongs of the unfortunate young man. Indeed, so entirely did he enter into John's case that John felt himself restored to hopeful life, half by the sympathy, and perhaps a little more than half by the genial absurdity that seemed to glide into everything from Montressor's devoted zeal. The light came back to the skies more completely in this humorous way than if some happy incident had restored it. He began to see through the exaggeration of his friend's feeling, that after all there was something laughable in his own despair, and that a man is not ruined in a moment in any such stagy and artificial way.

While this change began to operate, and while John poured forth his tale, he pursued the familiar way to his lodgings instinctively, leading the sympathetic Montressor with him without question asked. The actor had never before penetrated so far. It had not occurred to John to invite him, especially as he had never informed him of his real name. The fact that he had been so foolish as to call himself May to this early acquaintance had raised a barrier between them more effectual than any barrier of prudence or sense that such a friendship was not one to be cultivated. But in the fervour of his confidence, and in the enthusiasm of Montressor's sympathy, the consolation of it and the ridicule of it, everything else was forgotten. And John found himself at his own door with his faithful sympathiser before he was aware. He had opened it and bidden his friend to enter when his eye was suddenly caught by a slouching figure on the opposite side of the street, which aroused another set of feelings altogether. John thrust Montressor in, calling on him to sit down and wait, and then turning with a bound rushed across the street in the direction of this lounger, who, suddenly taking fright, had turned too, and was hurrying along as fast as a wavering pair of legs would carry him. The legs were unsteady, and little to be depended upon, though sudden panic inspired them, and they were worth nothing in comparison with youth and hot indignation now suddenly set on their track. The chase lasted but a minute. John made up to the fluttering, retreating figure, and was just about, with outstretched hand, to seize him, when the pursued suddenly turned round, meeting him with a rueful, deprecating, yet woefully smiling face, in which the same ridicule which had been rising in John's mind towards himself was blended with a sort of helpless despair and insinuating prayer for mercy.

'Stop,' cried his amanuensis, the traitor who had ruined him, with that rueful smile, 'I'll go with you anywhere—take me where you please. I—I can't defend myself.'

'What have you done with my papers?' cried John, trembling with hurry and rage, yet subdued, he could not tell how.

'I'll tell you,' said the other. 'I'll tell you everything. Take me somewhere and let me tell you.'

The young man laid his hand upon the old man's arm, and led him back, feeling somehow his heart melt towards the unresistant sinner. Montressor stood at the door watching this pursuit and capture. He waited for them as they came forward, his face expressing a sort of stupefication of wonder. John only remembered the spectator when he reached the door with his prisoner, and found this startled countenance confronting him.

'Why, May!' cried he, turning from one to another. 'Why, May!'

CHAPTER V.

THE CULPRIT.

JOHN'S amanuensis, whom he had so rashly trusted, had carried away his copy of John's scheme with, in reality, little or no idea of cheating, and none at all of injuring John. His faculties were confused by long courses of meditative sophistry, such as had been his amusement in the years when he had no other, and by the criminal atmosphere in which he had lived, in which the deception or spoiling of your neighbour was the most natural matter, the best sign of talent and originality, at once the excitement and the amusement of the perverted mind. The man who called himself March had a more than usual share of that confusion which so often accompanies breaches of the moral law. He had gone through far more than usual of those mental exercises by which all but the most stupid and degraded attempt to prove themselves right, or at least not so far wrong, in those offences which to the rest of the world are beyond excuse. And his mental ingenuity was such that he could make a wonderful plea to himself in favour of any course which fancy or temptation suggested. In the present case the effort had not been at all a difficult one. He had really meant no harm to John. He intended, in fact, to recommend John warmly, to put a good thing in his way. In all probability the young man would not prove a good advocate for himself. He might be shy of pushing his own interests: most inventors were shy and retiring, easily discouraged: and what he meant to secure would not in reality be more than a percentage on the trouble he would take in recommending John. A percentage—that was what in reality it would be—and well earned: for had he not been at the trouble of copying, and indeed adding something of his own to the young man's dry plans and calculations, besides the service he would do him in carrying his goods as it were to market and securing a sale for them, and a profitable job for their inventor. Nothing could be more self-evident than this. At the end he came to be quite sure that he was doing his young benefactor a real service, and that nothing in his conduct wanted excusing at all.

He was a little shaken, however, by his reception at the office of Messrs. Spender and Diggs, and by their instant recognition of John's name, and their curious questions on the subject. Had the plan been rejected by Barretts, they asked—and he did not even know what 'Barretts' meant. He was still more dismayed when he found (though he ought to have known very well it must be so) that no answer would be given him on the subject till the papers were examined, and that it would be necessary that Sandford should come himself to elucidate and explain them. There was quite a little excitement in the office, evidently, about Sandford's work and its presentation there. The partner who seemed to him to be Diggs (he could not tell why, from his appearance), came and looked over the shoulder of the partner who must be Spender, and one or two others were called into the council and questions asked as to whether young Sandford had left Barretts, whether there had been a quarrel, what had happened. The ignorance he showed about all this, brought suspicious looks upon him, looks which disturbed all his calculations: for it had never occurred to him that any suspicion could attach to him in respect of a document written in his own hand, and which by that very fact surely belonged to him, more or less. He was glad at last to get away, feeling a certain distrust involved in the questions that were addressed to him, and beginning to wonder what they could do to him if it were discovered to be without John's permission that the papers were brought here. Pooh! he said to himself, but only when he had got away—nothing could be done to him; it was no wrong to John or anyone. He had a right, a moral right, to the work of his own hands: and it was in kindness he had done it; kindness qualified by a percentage which is what the very best of friends demand.

But if he was disturbed and troubled by this *contretemps*, Joe, who was really throughout the matter his inspiring influence, was much more so. He was angry and disappointed beyond description. He had expected, being so much more ignorant than his principal, money immediate, a sum down, for the papers which young Sandford had said were his fortune. He was furious with the feebleness of his 'mate,' who had left those papers without getting anything for them.

'I'd not a' bin such a blooming fool,' said Joe, whose adjectives are generally left out in this record. 'I'd a' up and spoken. Money down or ye gets nothin' from me. Lor, if I had a 'ansom coat to my back like you, and could speak like as them swells would listen to me, d'ye think I'd a' come back empty-handed like that?'

March was still more confused by this vituperation. It was in vain, he knew, to convince Joe that such a rapid transaction was impossible in the nature of things, for neither Joe nor his kind know anything of the nature of things. They know that when they have anything to sell, money is to be got for it, and that is all. Joe made his patron and dependent (for the poor man was both) very uncomfortable on this subject: and other things too made him uncomfortable; the necessity for communicating with John, and informing him that he must see Spender & Diggs, and explain his scheme to them; and the necessity for going back to Spender & Diggs, which Joe had pressed upon him, incapable of hearing reason. What was he to do? The poor man hung about the street in which John lived, half hoping for an encounter which might clear up the matter one way or other. When he saw John his heart gave a jump of pleasure and relief in the first instance, and then the instinct of the offender came upon him and he turned and fled. But what was his flight worth before the pursuit of the active and impassioned youth who could have outstripped his swiftest pace in a stride or two? And then the fugitive said to himself that he was not really guilty, that he had done nothing to be afraid of. Kindness, qualified by a percentage. The rueful smile which was in his eyes when he turned to John was half conciliatory and half made up of self-approbation and amusement at the success of that phrase. Naturally, John was aware of neither of these sentiments. He pushed his prisoner before him into his sitting-room, taking no heed of the exclamations of Montressor. It was a trouble to him at all times to hear that name of May from the actor's lips, but it was his own fault, and he could blame nobody. He thrust the culprit into his sitting-room, and pushed him into a chair without saying a word. He was breathless, not with the exertion so much as with the tumult in his mind, the eagerness, and passion. He had not expected to find thus the means of exonerating himself so soon, nor could he help a certain blaze of wrath against the man who had done him so ill a turn.

'There!' he said, waving Montressor aside with his hand. 'Tell me first why you did it. What induced you to steal my papers and try to ruin me? Was not I kind to you?—was I not——'

'Steal your papers!' said the offender, with a look of surprised innocence. 'I stole none of your papers. The copy which I had myself made at your request was surely by all laws of reason mine in the first place, and not yours.'

John gazed at him with a gasp of astonishment at this extraordinary doctrine, but for the first moment found nothing to say.

'I allow,' said the culprit, with a certain magnanimity, 'that had I been engaged by you at, let us say, so much a day to make this copy, with a full understanding that it was to be your property, your question might be justified; but, as a matter of fact, no stipulations of the kind were made. You suggested to me that I should come here and copy your papers—with the benevolent intention of keeping me out of mischief—I suppose out of the company which you did not think good for me, of my faithful Joe.'

He had changed his position in the chair to a more easy one, and leaned forward a little, speaking, demonstrating slightly, easily, with his hand. John, in his sudden fury, and in the darkness of his distress, felt the current of his thoughts arrested, and his mind standing still with wonder. He gasped, but the words would not come.

'But there was no engagement,' resumed the speaker, with a smile; 'nothing was said about so much a day. My labour was not put to any price, nor was there any time mentioned when it should be finished, or anything said about its ultimate destination. You will see that I am quite exact when you think over the circumstances. Isn't it so? Well, then, by all laws of logic, the copy was mine, and I had a right to do what I liked with it; put it in the fire if I liked——'

'But not to offer my scheme, my work, my ideas to—to—another firm,' cried John, in his confusion: 'to an opposition—to a——'

He saw he had made a mistake, but in his excitement could not tell what it was.

'Oh,' said March, 'I see! Now I understand; it is a question of rivalry: they're competitors—they're on the other side? Certainly that wasn't at all what I intended: and now I understand.'

It was John's impulse to seize him by the collar, to shake the sophistry out of this bland usurper of his rights. But he did not do so. He restrained himself with a strong effort, and recovered the thread of reason which had been snatched for a moment out of his hand.

'We might go into that,' he said, 'if you had the least right to take from me what was my work, and not yours. But you are too clever not to see that this is quite a secondary question. Whatever you may say, you copied those papers for me, by my orders, for payment. Bah! what is the use of arguing about such a matter? You know it as well as I do. You know my papers are stolen, that you have tried to make a profit of them, that you have taken them from me, to whom they belonged——'

John's aspect in spite of himself was threatening: his countenance flushed, he changed his position, he clenched his hand. He was a powerful young man and the other was feeble and limp if not very old. Montressor, with his stage instinct, found it time for him to interfere.

'May,' he said, 'old friend, I have always stood up for you, though I know you've done a dark deed. I've spoken for you even to this brave boy. He's your own name, and may-be for aught I know he's your own flesh and blood. Oh, me old friend! there used to be a deal of good in you, though weak. How could you find it in your heart to do a wrong to a young beginner? That wasn't like what ye used to be, me old May——'

John had listened with a stupefied air to this speech. May! what did Montressor mean? He caught him by the arm.

'The man's name is March,' he said.

This brought, what all other accusations had not done, a faint colour to the culprit's face.

'One month's as good as another,' he said, with a feeble laugh, 'and begins with the same letter. So it's you, Montressor. I didn't notice who it was: the outer part of you is in better trim than when I saw you the other day.'

The actor replied, with a wave of his hand,

'What has to be thought upon at present,' he said, 'is you and not me.'

This was not the policy of the man who was on his trial.

'I suppose,' he said, 'it's the fortune of war. The other day I was able to help you as an old friend, and now it's you that patronise me.'

'May,' said John. He could not get beyond that point. What they said between themselves was nothing to him. He paid no attention to what they said. May! There swept into his mind a quick passing recollection of the feverish anxiety he had once felt to identify somehow and find out his relationship with some one of the name, and the Mayor of Liverpool, whom he had almost disturbed in his state to ask, Do you know anyone——? But he never met anywhere an individual who bore that name till now.

'Ye see before ye,' said Montressor, embarrassed, 'me young friend, the unfortunate man that I was trying to recommend to you the last time we met. He says true, he was better off at that moment than I was; but that makes no difference. Yes, me noble boy. This is the May I told ye of. I have thought there was a likeness in some things between ye; but me wife would not hear me say it, for, John May, ye have the heart of a king: and me poor friend there, though he's named the same——'

The man, who had not been listening any more than John had listened to the private conversation between his two companions, here woke up from his own thoughts with a slight start.

'Who,' he said, 'are you calling John May? My name is Robert, not John at all—if it is me you mean. My father's name was John, an honest worthy man. I always made up my mind to call the boy after him. What do you know about John May? that's not my name, not my name at all. I'm rather in a weak state of health and I can't bear very much. You wouldn't speak of such things if you knew that they threw me into a tremble all over, which is very bad for me. Who do you mean by John May?'

The three men looked at each other in a tremulous quiver of excitement, like the flashing of intense heat in the air. They gazed at each other saying nothing. Montressor, though he had hitherto been calm, was growing agitated too, he could not tell why. There was a suppressed excitement in the very air round them which none of the three could fully understand. At this moment there was a knock at the door, which they all heard, as if they heard it not, without an attempt to make any reply. The world outside was for the moment blank to them; they had something more important than anything outside to settle among themselves.

CHAPTER VI.

A CRISIS.

IT had been about noon when John left Messrs. Barretts' office. It was now between three and four in the afternoon. His long walk, his talk with Montressor, the agitation and excitement of the catastrophe had made the time go as upon wings. But it had not gone upon wings at the office, where there was a great deal of commotion and discomfort, the pupils saying among themselves that for Sandford to go away in such a way was next to impossible; that little Prince, the little sneak, had told some lie—just like him; that the bosses, or the governors, or whatever other name for the heads of the office happened to be current at the moment, had made a howling mistake, and that the whole affair was nothing but a proof of the general stupidity of those teachers and overseers whom it is the mission of youth to dethrone. This agitation of feeling was not confined to the pupil-room or the outer office. It entered in, with the most serious results, to the very sanctuary of the establishment, Mr. Barrett's own room, where Mr. William had a controversy with his father, which nothing but the decorum necessary between the heads of such a government could have kept within bounds.

Mr. Barrett was a pessimist by nature, and one who always expected to be deceived and wronged. He had heard, he forgot what, that had led him to expect evil of John, and to that idea he had clung during the period of the young man's training with the purest faith. He had to confess from time to time that John had done very well so far, but—— He never forgot to shake his head and add that but. Now he was, if it is permissible to say so of a good man, delighted that his prophecies were justified. He told his son that he had always expected it, 'from something his mother told me,'— though in the course of years he had forgotten what Mrs. Sandford had told him, which was not much.

William Barrett, however, was of another mind. He had liked John— he had put full faith in him, he had appreciated his practical abilities, and the good work he did, and his power of managing men, and had been disposed to look indulgently upon any theories or plans he might have. This was all the length his mind had gone when John spoke to him first of that scheme for draining the Thames Valley. He had smiled at it very good-humouredly—he had said to himself that when boys do take up an idea it is generally a magnificent one, but that it is better even to plan something on a ridiculously gigantic scale than to think of nothing at all. He was prepared, indeed, to get some amusement out of John's Thames Valley. Perhaps there might be something in it, some idea which a maturer brain could work out. There was no telling, but at all events it would be worth looking at for the fun of it, if nothing more: a youth of that age, with no experience to speak of, tackling a business which had baffled the wisest! But it was like a boy to do so. Fools rush in—or at least pupils rush in—where engineers sometimes fear to tread.

So he looked forward with amused expectation to the production of John's scheme. But when Prince told him that story of Spender & Diggs, the scheme took a different aspect in Mr. William Barrett's eyes. It gained an importance, a reality which nothing else could have given it. He did not smile at the idea of this absurd youthful plan as presented to the rival office. It became immediately a serious matter; a project of the greatest importance. All at once it became possible, very likely, that the other firm, who had nothing to do with John, might be about to reap all the benefit of him, and to enter upon the greatest engineering work that had been attempted for years, through this boy at whose plans 'Barretts' had smiled. William Barrett had no inclination to smile now. It was deadly earnest by this time: and he could not but feel sure in the natural certainty of events that this scheme which he had pooh-poohed would be seen in its true light by the others, and would make the fortune of Spender & Diggs.

This thought had made him severe to John, though not so severe as his father: and more open to conviction. His mind was at all times more open to conviction than that of his father: and when John had burst out of the office, in the first rage of his indignation, refusing to defend himself, Mr. William, as has been said, followed him to the door, calling him back, with a compunction which he could not get rid of. This compunction did nothing but go on increasing in the blank which followed that fiery scene. And the atmosphere in the pupil's room affected Mr. William, too, though he was not aware of it. He had a consciousness that the lads were saying among themselves, in the slang of which all elder persons disapprove, that the bosses had made a thundering mistake. Had they made a mistake? He was, in his heart, of the same opinion as the pupil-room. He did not think that John Sandford had done this thing. Now that the flurry of discovery was over, he asked himself was it likely? had the young fellow ever done anything that looked the least like it? Had he not always been as steady as a rock, always honest and true, never neglecting his employers' interests, carrying out their orders, as good a worker as could be? Was it likely he should turn round all at once? This thought worked in his mind silently, while those boys entertained each other with saying that the bosses had made a mistake: and it was greatly stimulated by the exasperating suggestion that Spender & Diggs might reap all the profit, and might go far ahead of

Barretts in the struggle for fortune and fame. Would they go ahead of Barretts? He began to remember John's start of surprise, his question as to who it was that had carried his papers to the other office, his look of enlightenment. If they had been stolen from him, and the papers which he had flung down on the table, were, as he had said, his original scheme, Spender & Diggs might not find it so easy to shoot ahead of Barretts. On the whole, thinking it over, it was more likely that Spender & Diggs had cheated than John. It would not be the first time. They might have put one of their men up to it, to find out what the young fellow was working at. Of course it soon got abroad among the lads what one was doing—and what more likely than that the rival firm, old hands at that sort of thing, people far more used to picking the brains of other people's pupils than to developing talent among their own, what if they had secured possession of the copy of John's scheme by one of the underhand ways with which they were familiar? On the whole, that was really more likely than that Sandford, a lad against whom nobody had a word to say, who had always behaved well, should have gone over, without rhyme or reason, to the enemy.

By dint of long-continued reasonings like this, William Barrett worked himself up by the time he left the office to seek another interview with John. He said to himself that he would put his pride in his pocket, and go after the young fellow, who no doubt was miserable, though he had so much pluck he would not show it. His heart smote him that he had not taken all these things into consideration before, and he had visions of young Sandford's misery and despair, which affected even the middle-aged imagination of a man quite unused to anything heroical. He felt that his father had been unkind to John, which gave him at once an impulse and a motive for seeking the young man out—for, though he respected his father, the junior partner was generally more or less in opposition to him. All these things together made him determine to go after John, and have it out with him. He got his address almost stealthily, as not wishing anyone in the office to know until he saw what would come of it, and set out from the office a little earlier than usual that no time might be lost. He found the door open when he came to the house, and being himself somewhat excited, and beyond the rule of common laws, went in without ringing the bell; and, hearing voices in the first sitting-room he came to, knocked at the door. He was thus brought into the very midst of the agitated group which we have attempted to set before the reader at the climax of their excitement. The voices ceased, after a moment, but no attention was paid to Mr. Barrett's knock. Something of the excitement that was in the air communicated itself to him.

'Sandford,' said William Barrett, putting his head in at the door.

They were all silent, staring at each other full of confused trouble, suspicion, and uncertainty. Even John felt vaguely, when the original question rose up before him in the sudden apparition of Mr. William Barrett's grave face, that another matter had since arisen which swallowed up the first. The intruder who came in without invitation, feeling somehow that here was a crisis above conventional rules found that the interest centred like the high light in a picture in the countenance of the man who sat at the table, leaning on it, his whole person quivering with a tremulous movement like palsy, his face turned, pale, with a half-anxious, half-fatuous beseeching smile upon it to the other man standing opposite to him, who on his side looked from John to the new-comer and back again with a look of amazement and confusion. John himself stood half-stupefied between them, giving no more than a glance of recognition to his employer, occupied with more urgent affairs; and yet Mr. Barrett had good reason to know that his own mission to this youth who was so strangely daring his fate, was in one sense life and death.

'Whom do you mean by John May? John May's not a common name, neither is Sandford. Montressor, you're stirring up all my life, and you know it. Most things I can bear well enough. I've gone through a great deal. I'm hardened to most things—but not—not—to my little boy's name. You've got a child of your own, and you ought to know. I've not seen that little chap for fourteen years. I don't know where he is now, if he's living or if he's dead, and yet once he was the apple of my eye. Montressor, what do you mean with your play-acting and your stage tricks, bandying about what was the name of my little boy?'

John Sandford stood listening to these words which came out, with pauses between, in a voice which was full of real feeling, a voice so different from the easy sophistry, the humorous self-contempt, the confused philosophy which were its usual utterance—with sensations indescribable, and something like a moral overturn of his whole being: vague recollections, suggestions from the past, horrible fears, doubts, certainties, confusion, rose up in him, enveloping him like a mist. He cared no more for William Barrett than if he had been an office-boy; he forgot all the question about the Thames Valley. These things, though he had felt them half-an-hour ago to be the most momentous in the world, departed from him as if they had never been. He stood, scarcely able to see for the haze of feverish excitement that had got into his eyes, staring blindly, with all his faculties concentrated in that of hearing, listening for what would come next.

'Sir,' said Montressor, 'ye do me wrong. The drama is the drama, and I love it; but stage business is not, as ye say, for common life. Me own name I don't deny, if all were laid bare, is perhaps not Montressor. But the poor player is likewise a man. Had I any stage effect in me mind when I told ye there was one of your own name I would recommend ye to? here he stands, and a young fellow any man might be proud of. The first time I set eyes on him he saved me chyild's life—judge if I was likely to forget his name. This, me poor friend, is John May.'

'That's nonsense as I can testify,' said William Barrett, breaking in bluntly. 'I don't know who your friends are, Sandford, and perhaps I ought to beg your pardon for interfering; but you're very young though you're not perhaps aware of it. Come, gentlemen, if you've got any hold upon this young man I shall be glad to answer your questions about him, and let him attend to his business. He is in fact my pupil, and it's not to my interest his mind should be disturbed from his work. Whatever stories you may have heard I must know more about him than you do. His name is Sandford. He was placed by his mother in our hands.'

'Sir,' said Montressor, with dignity, 'these are me friends, both the young man and the old. I do not turn to strangers to ask for information concerning me friends. Ye may be well meaning, but ye are ignorant—and I find ye intrusive,' said the actor, turning away with a wave of his hand.

'Sandford!' cried William Barrett. Capitals could not do justice to the injured majesty of this cry. Intrusive! In the rooms of a pupil taken without a premium (that even he remembered in the shock of the indignity), such a word to be applied to him!

But John said nothing. He was stupefied, or mad, or drunk, which was it? He scarcely gave his employer a look. The colour had disappeared from his face, his eyes seemed to have a film over them, his lips trembled. He said at last, almost inaudibly, looking straight before him at vacancy,

'My real name is John May—that was my name when I was a child— the other—is my grandfather's name.'

Then the man who had injured John, who had taken his plans from him and robbed him, and made him appear a traitor, rose up tottering, supporting himself by the table.

'If it's your grandfather's name,' he said, 'and you were Johnnie May when you were a child—— God help us all, it's fourteen years ago. Are you my little chap, my little man, that I used to take out of your bed in your nightgown, with your bonny bright eyes shining? Oh, God in heaven, I'm not fit to be any good lad's father. Are you my little boy? Are you Johnnie May?'

The room and all that was in it swam in dark circles of confusing mist in John's eyes. He grasped a chair to support himself, to defend himself; the floor seemed to give way under his feet.

'I'll—I'll come back presently,' he said.

Mr. Barrett thought more and more, with a grieved heart, that the young fellow must have been drinking, as with a sudden rush he gained the door, and clung to that again for a moment, like a man who has no control of his limbs or movements. There he paused, and, looking at them, said,

'Wait: wait here: till I come back——'

Mr. Barrett followed him quickly, afraid of what might follow. He found John ghastly and helpless, sitting on the step of the outer door. The young man gave a little nod of his head.

'Wait,' he gasped, 'I'll be better—in a moment—I want a little air.'

'Sandford, what is the matter? Something has happened to you; what are you going to do?'

John did not answer for a minute. He sat with his mouth open taking long breaths, as if the air had been a cordial which he was gulping down in mouthfuls. The street was very quiet, there was nobody in sight, and the air of early summer was fresh and a little chill in afternoon greyness. Presently the young man rose and smiled faintly at his companion.

'I'm better,' he said. 'I'm fit now for what I've got to do.'

'Tell me, Sandford, what is it you are going to do? Nothing desperate, I hope. I came to tell you I was ready to hear any explanation—'

John waved his hand with an air of almost derision.

'Do you suppose I'm thinking of that? It's gone far beyond that.'

'What can be beyond that?' cried the employer, with exasperation. Then he seized the young man by the arm. 'What are you going to do?'

'I am afraid I must have a cab,' said John, with his confused look, 'for quickness; besides that I couldn't walk. All my strength's gone out of me.'

'But what are you doing? What has happened? Where are you going now?' John looked at his chief, the friend of so many years, with a piteous smile.

'I am going to find out—if there's any hope for me—what's to become of me,' he said.

CHAPTER VII.

MRS. SANDFORD'S VIEW.

MRS. SANDFORD sat in her matron's room in the light of the bay windows, making up her accounts as usual. She was regulating the lists of linen in the hospital, the surgical appliances, the provisions of all kinds. Her round of the wards had been made. The nurses had given their reports, the special cases had been visited. Her day's work, so to speak, was done. The afternoon was the time for rest. She was occupying it, as she often did, in this necessary, but not ostentatious work, upon which so much of the comfort of the little community devoted to healing and merciful service, depended. Mrs. Sandford was known to be a great administrator: nothing was ever wanting, nothing to seek, under her management; her stores never ran out. But she was so used to this work of regulation and oversight that she did not find it very interesting. Sometimes she would lay down her pen, sometimes even lean back in her chair, which was not, however, a seductive lounge, but an ample, comfortable Chippendale, in which you sat upright very much at your ease, but had no encouragement to loll. She had things to think of apart from the hospital. A letter lay on her table among all her lists and account-books, which was from Susie, and there were things in it which made this mother, who, after all, though perhaps of sterner fibre than most, was still of the same stuff from which ordinary mothers are made—both smile and sigh. Susie's life was undergoing new developments. A certain commotion was in it of new forces awakening, and new thoughts. Perhaps, under the most favourable circumstances, Susie was not likely to make such revelations as would justify any critic in saying that she was 'in love'; but there were in her letter indications, little eddies which proved how the current went, straws that showed how the wind was blowing. For one thing, she kept up a continual comparison between two unknown persons, of which she herself was evidently unconscious, but which her mother perceived gradually by dint of repetition. 'Mr. Percy Spencer tells me'—'but Mr. Cattley says:'—she had told her mother at first all about her visitors, and how these two came and went, and talked of John. Susie had a great deal to say, too, of Elly, and had made her mother aware of all that had gone on in that respect, and also of Mrs. Egerton and her opposition, which by times extended to Susie and by times ebbed away altogether, as circumstances, or humour, or the weather moved the parish queen in one way or another. Those reports were always quite simple, and often amusing, for Susie had a quiet way of telling a story, very circumstantial and clear, which sometimes gave her readers a more luminous and humorous view than she was herself aware of. But Susie made no comparison in respect to the ladies of Edgeley. Their intercourse with her was simple. It was her visitors of the other sex who evidently produced this effect of balance and comparison in her mind.

'Mr. Percy gave me his view of it; he takes very strong views; but Mr. Cattley tells me——'

This was always the position in which these two appeared—Percy bringing forward all kinds of opinions, decisive of many matters, social and otherwise; but Mr. Cattley always adding a criticism or comment, something that changed the issue. Mrs. Sandford, for the fiftieth time, leaned back in her chair, and put down her pen, and asked herself, with a faint, lingering smile, which softened her stern face, what Susie meant. Susie was her own child, to whom her heart was soft, her companion, the sharer of all her thoughts. The sternness which she had shown to John had never touched his sister. Susie knew her mother entirely, knew what she meant, and what her past life had been. There were no secrets between these two. Of many things in his own antecedents, John was ignorant, but Susie knew everything. All Susie's ways of thinking had grown under her mother's eye. She had never thoroughly known her son, but she knew Susie through and through. This made the greatest difference in their mutual relations. Mrs. Sandford was to her daughter both tender, and soft, and gentle. Susie knew how to make her laugh, to bring tears to her eyes, whereas to John there was no laughter in her. All this, and even the contrast with John, who was in no such position, drew the mother and daughter more closely together. And it was with all the mingled sympathy and alarm, and tender prescience and pleasure, and regret of that relationship, that she saw the moment coming when the child would find some one else to be nearer to her, more a portion of herself and her life than even her mother.

Mrs. Sandford felt, with that exquisite fellow-feeling which is like divination, almost before Susie did, the development of a new affection in Susie's soul. And she leaned back in her chair between happiness and sadness, pleased to see her girl 'respected like the lave,' though already conscious of the desolation that desirable and good thing would bring with it—asking herself, almost with amusement, Which would it be? It was a mood more soft than was at all usual with her, and, notwithstanding the darkness that must come with the fulfilment of those dreams, it was a happy mood. That her mild Susie should have, not one but two suitors flattered and amused her. Which would it be? Mr. Cattley, in his mild, middle age, or Percy, the young priest, who had never intended to yield to the weakness of love-making? This was the subject of Mrs. Sandford's thoughts: and other matters more painful, if any painful matters were at that moment within the possibilities of her life, had floated away like clouds from the languid sweetness of the afternoon sky.

There was something, however, in the sound of the hurried step she heard approaching which roused her. It rang along the unoccupied passages, quick, eager, hurried, yet with a little stumble of weakness in it, as of excitement gone too far, and losing hold of itself. She listened, and instantly sat upright in her chair, and put Susie's letter away under a bundle of papers. It was perhaps something very bad brought into the accident ward, or the man in No. 4 had been taken with another attack, or—— Then something made her start a little.

'It is his step,' she said to herself: and *he* was John, the boy as she always called him in her heart.

He pushed open the door without knocking, and saying hurriedly, 'May I come in,' came in without waiting for permission. Her experienced eye saw at once that he had received a great shock. Either in body or mind he had been shaken violently. His hair hung in damp masses on his forehead. He was without colour, save when in speaking he suddenly reddened and then was pale again. A touch of personal disarrangement made this agitation of his appearance more remarkable. His tie had got loose, and he had not perceived it. Such a simple matter of external appearance seems to set a seal upon the profoundest commotions of life.

She cried out, 'What is the matter?' before he could speak a word. Then, starting suddenly with that instinctive alarm which moves us for those we love, added quickly, 'Susie! You have had some bad news.'

'Not of Susie,' he said, in a breathless way. 'Mother, I have come for you. Come with me instantly, for God's sake!'

'What is the matter, John? I can't go out like this, you know. I have to make arrangements. What is it?—for heaven's sake tell me what it is.'

'I may never in my life ask such a thing from you again. Most likely I shall never want it. If you have any feeling for me, for God's sake come with me. To me it is life or death.'

She put her hand upon his arm, and drew him towards her, looking in his face, feeling with a professional touch his hands and the throbbing of his pulse.

'Something has gone amiss,' she said. 'Your hands are cold, and yet your pulse is high. You have had some shock.' She got up as she spoke, and made him sit down in her chair, and put her hands upon his head. 'Tell me what is the matter,' she said, in that tone of mild determination with which she overawed her patients. 'You are not fit to be flying about.'

There was something in the touch, in the maternal authority—though that was scarcely more individual to him than to any other—which touched the poor young fellow in the feverish crisis of feeling in which he was. It was a relief to sink down into the chair, to feel even its wooden arms giving him a sensation of support. And to have some one to fall back upon at such a moment was the best thing in heaven or earth. He had never wanted such a prop before. It was against all the principles of his life to look for it, and yet there was the profoundest consolation in it. He closed his eyes for a moment, and the heat and the horror of his thoughts relaxed a little. He had meant to seize upon her, to carry her away in a whirlwind of passionate haste and anxiety, to confront her with *him*, the stranger who had possession of John's rooms, and seemed to claim possession of his life. That had seemed at first the only thing to do: to carry her off without warning, to bring her face to face with that unthought of, unsuspected apparition, and demand of her, 'Who is this?' Perhaps there had been in it a gleam of personal vengeance too, the desire to recompense with a keen, swift stroke of punishment the deception put upon him, and all the mysteries now suddenly let loose upon his head. But the touch of his mother's hand, the anxiety in her voice, the kindness—though perhaps no more than any patient at the hospital would have called forth—over-turned all these intentions in a moment. He was wound up to such a passion of feeling that everything told upon him, and the revulsion was great. He leaned back, touching her shoulder, laying his head upon it.

'Mother,' he said, like a child, with a pathetic voice of reproach, 'why did you tell me he was dead?'

'John!' she started so violently that the pillow of rest on which he had leaned seemed to reject as well as fail him. 'John!'

He turned round upon her suddenly, and caught her hands in his.

'Mother,' he said again, 'is it true? Mother, is it true? I have never understood. God help me, was this what it meant all the time?'

Mrs. Sandford, who was so self-controlled and so strong, trembled and quivered in his hold. She said, in a hoarse whisper,

'What has happened? Tell me what it is.'

He held her hands fast, and would not let her go, swaying a little backward and forward as if he were shaking her, though he had no such meaning.

'I have never understood,' he repeated. 'I must have been told what was not true. Now I know: you ought all to have seen that I must be told sooner or later. Is *that* true?'

She was a woman of great resolution, and she freed herself from him, though his hold was so close. She came round to the other side of the table, and stood looking at him, with the steady look which had daunted many a rebel. She said,

'You are ill; you don't know what you are saying. I should not wonder if you had had a slight sunstroke. You must go to Susie's room, which is cool and fresh, and lie down.'

And then there ensued a moment's parley, but not with words—with keen eyes looking into each other across the table. She stood as steady as a rock, as if she were thinking of nothing but the accidental illness of which she spoke. But John saw that the lighter part of her, the edge, so to speak, the line of her black gown, the turn of her elbow, had a quiver in them. He saw this without knowing that he saw it, as we do in moments of emotion.

'Mother,' he said, 'it's no mistake; it's not illness. It's what I tell you. Come with me and see him: and if you can say then that it is not true—— Ah!' he exclaimed, with a sharp tone of distress, 'you can't. I see it in your face.'

Mrs. Sandford did all she could to steady herself still.

'To see whom?' she said. 'To see——' Then, with a long-drawn breath, 'You are trying to frighten me. I know—no one of whom you can be speaking.'

'Then why are you afraid?' he said.

She kept standing, gazing at him for a moment more. Then a sort of shivering seized her, and in a moment all her defences seemed to fail. She gave him a look of agonised appeal, then came to him like a child flying from a suddenly realised danger, and dropped down by the side of his chair.

'Oh, John,' she cried, clinging to him, 'save me. I cannot see him— oh, no, no! You don't know what you ask. Say I am dead. Say I am—— Kill me rather, kill me! It would be kinder. Oh, no, no, no! I cannot, I cannot. I'll rather die. Save me, John!'

A horrible dismay crept through and through him as he bent over her, exclaiming, 'Mother, mother!' trying to soothe her—but above all a profound, all-subduing pity. He had his answer; there was no possibility of misunderstanding what this meant: but the sight of the convulsed and broken figure clinging to him in utter self-abandonment penetrated to his very heart. He clasped with his own the hands that held his arm. He put down his head to the face which, full of mortal terror and misery, looked up to him imploring his protection. His protection! for her so strong, so self-sufficing, so immovable. To see her at his feet was more than he could bear.

'Mother, I will; as far as I can, by every means I can. I will, I will—mother, it breaks my heart to see you. Then it is true, all true?'

And on the other side there seemed to rise before him another picture: the man with his smile arguing the question, persuading himself that anything he had done was, if not wholly right, at least far from being wrong, that it was the thing most natural to be done—with his air of mental confusion, yet satisfaction, his amiability, his conciliatory looks, his humorous self-consciousness, the subtle semi-intoxication which seemed to have got into his character. These things had made John smile a short time ago; they had filled him with a sort of compassionate kindness, an amused toleration of all the ways of this strange specimen of what human nature could come to. He was not amused or tolerant now. He thought with shrinking of this new, never-realised, impossible agent who had come into his life, impossible, yet, alas! real, never to be ignored again. But the first thing was his mother, his mother who, their positions reversed in a moment, clung to him with that face full of panic and anguish, flinging herself upon his protection. She, who was so strong, the embodiment of self-reliance and authority, to see her as weak as water, as weak as any poor woman, imploring her son to save her! He had never in his life till now given her more than the conventional kiss which their relationship seemed to demand when they met and parted. But now he held her close and kissed over and over again the white, agonised face which was pressed against his arm. Presently he raised her up tenderly and restored her to her seat—where gradually her panic calmed down, and she was able to speak. But it was very terrible and strange to John that she asked no questions, but took the miserable fact for granted, as if it were a thing that must have happened, that she had expected sooner or later, something inevitable in her way.

'The only thing is,' he said, with a sigh of subdued impatience, 'why did you not tell me, mother. Why didn't I know?'

His question brought the shivering back, but she replied, with an effort,

'How can I tell you? We thought it was better so. I would not have you exposed to that knowledge. You were so young—and then it might never have been necessary—it might never have come——'

'You mean that he might have died—there?'

'It would,' she said, bowing her head, 'have been better so.'

'Without anyone to stand by him or say a word, without love or succour,' he cried. Was there not another side to the question? He thought she drew herself away from him with a renewed movement of alarm, and he rose from her side, too pitiful to be indignant, his heart wrung with contending thoughts.

She held out her hands to him with another outcry of terror.

'Don't go! I have no one. Don't forsake me, don't leave me alone! John, John!'

'I must,' he said, 'if I am to defend you, to save you, as you say. And then,' he added, 'there is more than that: to take care of—him. He cannot be ignored, mother; at least he has claims upon me.'

'Oh, John! Stay with me, don't go. It has not been for myself I have feared most, but for you. It was always for you that I have feared, lest he might get an influence, lest he might—— John, stay with me! Have I not the best right to you? I that have——'

'Distrusted me always, mother. I don't blame you, but you know it has been so.'

She covered her face with her hands.

'I am but a feeble, prejudiced woman. I claim no exception. I do wrong trying to do right, like all the rest, John. I feared, God forgive me, that you might turn out—I thought you were——'

'The son of my father,' he said, with a mingling of sweetness and bitterness which gave something keen and poignant to the sound of his voice. 'And so I am—and so I must prove myself now.'

CHAPTER VIII.

THE CONVICT.

WHEN John rushed away in the manner that has been described, Montressor and the other were left together looking at each other blankly. They said nothing so long as the sound of voices without betrayed that he was still there. They sat listening, looking at each other, in silence, till the sound of his footsteps had died away upon the stony pavement, and the quiet street had relapsed into its usual stillness. The look which they exchanged was like that of two convicted criminals waiting breathless till the steps of the avenger had died away. Montressor, at least, had done the young fellow no wrong, but he felt that he had somehow unconsciously, involuntarily, been the means of bringing trouble upon him. He felt like a culprit whispering to his fellow-conspirator when he said,

'May,' in a low voice, as if he might be overheard, 'what does it all mean?'

May looked up at him from where he sat by the table, leaning his forehead upon his hands. He shook his head, but he did not make any reply.

'May, we're old friends. I never turned me back upon ye, though many did. I've always felt an interest in where ye were, and how your time was running on. I hadn't much in me power, but many didn't do that.'

'Nobody did it,' said May. 'I'm like a martyr, a saint, in that, if in nothing else, Montressor; everyone forsook me. I had not a soul to inquire whether I was living or dead, but you.'

'Hush, May, me poor fellow!—your wife and family——'

'Do you know what they did? They disappeared, and left no sign of themselves anywhere. They must have changed their name; they sent a sum of money for me, but not a word. I came out not knowing if anyone belonging to me was living or dead, or where they were, or what had become of them. My wife may be at the end of the world for anything I know.'

'May be dead,' said the other, 'that's more likely.'

The convict shook his head.

'It must have been she who sent me the money. I had a mind not to take it at first. Like a bone to a dog to keep him from following you. I thought for half-an-hour I wouldn't take it: but after all,' he said, with a low laugh, 'money's not a bad thing in itself. It's a make-up for many things—when you can get nothing else.'

'Me poor soul! if you've sinned you've suffered,' said Montressor, with a sigh of sympathy.

The other laughed again.

'There's something to be said on both sides. What's sin? It's a thing that takes different aspects according to your point of view. And you may say what's suffering too? That is a pang to one person which would be the course of nature to another. My friend Joe never expected to have any welcome on the other side of the gates at Portland; not he. He was content to get out of it, to go where he pleased, to get drunk comfortably next night with nobody to interfere. He had no ridiculous expectations. What you call suffering to me was bliss to Joe.'

Montressor did not know what to reply; nothing in his own life, and not all the expedients of the theatre could furnish him with a fit answer. He tried to throw into his face and the solemn shake of his head, something which he ought to feel.

'All other things are according to your point of view,' the other went on; 'but money's absolute. It's always a good thing in its way. I took it, and I consoled myself that on the whole—that on the whole—— But children have a droll sort of hold upon you,' he said, quickly, with a broken laugh. 'I always felt I'd give a great deal to know what had become of my little boy.'

Montressor stretched out his hand, and took hold of May's across the table. Both nature and the theatre helped him here.

'Me poor friend!' he said.

'He was a delightful little chap. It might be because I was partial, you know—but I think there never was a finer little chap. I used to go upstairs, when I came in late, and fetch him out of his bed, out of his sleep, his mother said, and looked death and destruction at me—but it never did him any harm. I shouldn't wonder if he remembered it now. I think I see him in his white nightgown, with his two eyes shining, his hair all ruffled up, his little bare feet.' His voice ran off in a low, sobbing cough. 'I never saw such a little chap:—never a bit afraid, though I wasn't very steady sometimes when I carried him downstairs.'

There was a pause. Montressor had no stage precedent before him to teach him how to act in such an extraordinary crisis: but Nature began to make a hundred confused suggestions, which at first he could scarcely understand. The stillness seemed to throb and thrill around them, when this monologue ceased, demanding something from the actor, he could not tell what; some help which he did not know how to give, scarcely what it was.

'Me poor friend!' he said once more. 'You've done wrong, but wrong has been done to you. And this little chap, ye think ye've found him? Ye think he's turned out to be this—this noble young fellow here? If ye have an interest in him one way, I've got an interest in him in another, for he saved the life of me chyild—of me Edie,' the actor added, as in the theatre he would have said these touching words, 'who is the prop of me old age, and the pillar of me house.'

May, who had been roused out of his musings by the question, fell back into them as Montressor prolonged his speech, and now made no reply. The other continued:

'Me interest in him is strong. I'd save him any trouble, or disturbance, or distress—anything that was to humble him, or to shame him, or to put a stop to him making his way. I'd do that, whatever it might cost me—that I would, for me chyild's sake.'

'Your chyild?' said May, with an imitation of the actor's pronunciation, which Montressor scarcely perceived, but which tickled the speaker in the extraordinary lightness of his heart or temper. He laughed, and then took up the conversation, changing his tone.

'A child's a strange thing. It's yourself in a kind of way, and yet it's nicer than yourself. The naughtier it is, the nicer it is. It's endless fun. I don't know,' he said, with a wave of his hand, 'what the relationship is when it exists between you and somebody that, so to speak, is as old as yourself.'

'Me poor May! but that's a thing that can't be.'

'Myself, for instance,' continued the philosopher. 'I'm father to a child, not to a man. My little chap, if he had lived, would be—— I don't know,' he added, after a pause, 'that I'd be very sorry to hear he had died.'

'Hush, May!' said the other, with an outcry of dismay. 'I wouldn't believe ye. Ye can't mean it, whatever ye may say.'

'Why can't I mean it? My little chap belongs to me, whatever happens. He had always a smile and a kiss for his father; he was never afraid of me; he never looked at me stern, like his mother. Now, if he should happen to have grown into—something like this young fellow here——'

'Ye would be a lucky man, not a luckier man in all England: a brave boy of whom any father might be proud.'

'Ah!' said the vagrant, with a long-drawn breath, which ended in a faint laugh, 'and would he, do you think, be proud of me?'

There was another silence, for Montressor was daunted, and felt once more that even the resources of his profession failed him; and May went on, after the telling interval of that pause.

'A young fellow that is the pink of respectability, that never took a drop too much, nor went an inch out of the way in all his life! Lord, Montressor, think what it would be to be set down for life, to be overlooked by a fellow like that! to see in his eyes what he thought of you! I'm a poor wretch that can't live without a laugh. I couldn't, you know, if I were, as people used to say, within the ribs of death. I've made the best of things, and reasoned them out, and got a little fun out of them wherever I was. I know what would happen well enough. When I talked to him the other day, I was a sort of a strange beast to him that he was very sorry for. It nearly brought the tears into his eyes to hear me talk. I could almost tell you what he was thinking. "Poor beggar!" he was thinking, "it's all wrong and horrible, but if it gives him a little consolation in his misery——" He was awfully kind.'

'He's the kindest heart I ever came across,' cried the actor, with an exaggeration which was very allowable in the circumstances, 'and liberal as the day, and never forgets a friend.'

This May dismissed again with a wave of his hand as something outside of the question.

'He was awfully kind. It looked like what you call the voice of nature on the stage, Montressor. One doesn't often come across it anywhere else. Do you know he picked me up dr—— well, as the policemen say, a little the worse for liquor—in the street? Think of it, a young man that is the flower of respectability—that never consorted with the wicked. And after seeing me unadorned like that, and knowing where I came from, which Joe did his best to publish, taking me in, establishing me here, and giving me his papers to copy! By the way, I'm a little sorry about these papers,' he went on. 'Perhaps it was stretching a point to take them away—convey the wise it call—though they weren't his, strictly speaking, you know; he hadn't paid for them or made any bargain; but still a Puritanical person might say—— It was all that sophist Joe, a casuist born, though he doesn't know a rule of logic. And then the ridiculous name of those engineer people caught my fancy. Spender & Diggs, don't you know; it's grotesque. That tempted me. But, perhaps, after all, it was stretching a point—the jury might say it was a breach of trust. I think I'll go and get them back.'

'Me friend!' cried Montressor, 'there I see ye as I always liked to see ye—generous, whatever else.'

'Yes,' said May, with some complacency, 'I flatter myself I always was that; but few people knew the line to take with me. The talk has always been about justice. As if justice was a thing to be defined! If every man had his deserts, which of us would be uppermost, I wonder? Not those fellows in scarlet that sentence other men, or the pettifogging shopkeepers on a jury that know about as much of justice—— I think I'll go and get those papers back.'

'Come on; I'll go with ye—I'll stand by ye in a righteous cause!' cried Montressor, starting to his feet.

'Gently,' said May, looking at him with mild eyes, leaning back in his chair. 'It's too late to-day. I'll go to-morrow as soon as I'm up; and as for that old casuist Joe——'

'What's Joe, or any other man,' said Montressor, 'in comparison with what's generous, me friend, and kind? Here's a young man, and as fine a young man as ye'll see, that's been good to ye—even if there's nothing more in it.'

'Even if there's nothing more in it,' said May, in his mellow, melting voice. 'And there may be more in it, Montressor. There may be little Johnnie in it, God bless him, my nice little chap!'

'Me friend,' said Montressor, with enthusiasm, 'there may be little Johnnie in it, grown up to be a credit to all that belongs to him, to be the prop of your old age and the blessin' of your life, like me own Edie—to thank ye for saving him from ruin, to bless ye——'

'Hold hard!' said the other. 'Montressor, my good fellow, your eloquence is carrying you away. Thank me for saving him from ruin! It was hauling me up for stealing his papers that he was thinking of——'

'But not,' cried John's advocate, 'not since he knew—not since it began to dawn upon him, poor boy——'

The convict put out his hand—and the actor stopped short in his appeal. They sat silent once more, looking at each other with thoughts that were too deep for speech. It was May who took up the broken sentence at last.

'Ay,' he said, 'when it began to dawn upon him, poor boy, that the man he had picked up out of the streets, the man he had been so charitable to, the man he had trusted and that had betrayed him, the convict from Portland, was his father! Good Lord! Think of this happening to a proud, virtuous, self-conceited, right-minded, well-behaved young prig like that!' He burst into something that sounded like a laugh, and yet was more miserable than any outcry of despair. 'Think of that, Montressor,' he said again, after a moment. 'That's stranger than any of your stage effects. Poor young beggar! all made up of pride and honour and rectitude, and all that, and as ambitious as Alexander to boot.' He got up for a moment and stood by the table and looked round him. 'I think I'll go away. I think I'll go right away and take myself out of the boy's road. What would be the good of torturing him, and making him try to be respectful to his father? He'd be respectful—and awfully disagreeable,' he added, with a lighter laugh. 'I'll not wait for him any longer. I'll go right away.'

'Me noble friend! it's your true heart that speaks!' cried Montressor, seizing him by the arm. 'Me house is open to you, May, and me heart—come with me.'

May looked round upon the room, the fire of his sentiment dying out, the habitual twinkle coming back to his eye.

'It's a dreadfully respectable little place,' he said. 'Tidy—not a thing out of order. Could you imagine a comfortable pipe and glass here? And I know how he would look at me. It makes a difference when it's a relation. A poor man off the streets is the sort of thing you can be kind to without derogation—but not a—father. I'm not the sort of father for a man. A little boy like my little chap wouldn't mind; but a fine, respectable young man! And women don't mind so much—that is, some women. How old is your Edie, Montressor, and what sort of a girl?'

'Sixteen, and an angel,' said the actor, 'and dances like one: and she's the prop of me house.'

'Sixteen—you must take me to Edie. Sixteen's too young to ask many questions: and when it dances besides! But you've got a wife?'

'She's an angel too, May.'

'It's you that are lucky, Montressor. I wonder if I've still got a wife? She was a sort of an arch-angel, don't you know, too high-minded, too grand for the like of me. I wonder if she's alive. Yes, she must be alive. Nobody but she would have sent me that money without a word. Perhaps, Montressor, it's her he's gone to consult.'

'Never mind, me friend. Let's think no more of them. Let's go away.'

'It will be so,' said May, as if speaking to himself; 'his mother—that master of his said. Confound all jealous masters, he will cause me a deal of trouble getting those things back. Ay, the mother! she'll tell him everything, she'll not spare the old riotous good-for-nothing—his father!' Here the voice changed. 'A father like me,' he added, 'isn't for a young man, Montressor; you're right in what you say. I'd do for a boy, a little fellow like my own little chap. He and I could go away together where nobody ever heard of us. Get a little farm in the country, perhaps, and a spade, and—that sort of thing: and the poor little beggar would never know. But for a man that is respectability itself, and all that—— No, no, you're right, Montressor. Take me to your angel that dances, and the other one—what does she do?—perhaps she sings.' He burst forth into a tremulous, broken laugh. 'Two angels—instead of my own little chap. You're right, Montressor. Don't let us wait for the poor boy that's coming back broken-hearted. Who knows, if I weren't such a good-for-nothing, if I weren't such a reckless fool, I might be broken-hearted too.'

'Me poor friend!' the actor cried, 'as long as I have a roof over me head, come; it's but a poor place, but ye'll be welcome. Montressor's door is never shut against trouble and sorrow. And when ye see me Edie dance—and she'll dance to ye as if ye were a crowned head—ye'll forget everything.'

'Ah, I'll forget everything,' said the other; he added, musing, 'I'll do that easy, whether or no.'

CHAPTER IX.

THE FIRST SHOCK.

JOHN left the hospital, he scarcely knew when, and could not tell how. He had forgotten, though he never could for a moment forget, that he had left waiting for him the two men, the man who—— Remember him!—it seemed to John an impossibility that ever again, even if he lived a hundred years, he could forget what had been revealed to him that day, or the look of the man's face, who suddenly in a moment had lifted the veil of his own childish life, and made the playful, sweet recollection which had never died out of his mind an instrument of torture.

He was conscious when he came out from under the shadow of the great building in which his mother's life was spent, and found himself on the bridge with the clear vacancy of the river on each side of him, that the afternoon had waned, that the sun was going down, and that a sentiment of the coming evening, with its rest and quietness, was already in the air. But that a long time had elapsed since in hot haste and excitement he had crossed that bridge, going to demand from his mother an explanation of this horror, he could not tell. It was a moment, an age, he could not tell which. Despair had been in his soul, mingled with a passionate determination that this thing should not be, when he went: but he was still and silent as he returned. He had not received either explanation or proof. His mother's panic was proof enough on one side, as were the few words that he had said on the other. These words alone were unanswerable, unforgettable. If the convict had vanished from his eyes unnamed, John felt that his fond recollection of that child in his night-gown was enough to have proved all the terrible story. For who could know it but himself and one other, himself and his father?

His father! What a name that was, full of tenderness, full of honour, a name that could neither be obliterated nor transferred, nor lost in forgetfulness. A man's father is his father for ever, whatever circumstances may arise. John, the son of——: is not that the primitive description, the first distinction of every man, the thing which gives him standing among his fellows? The mother may or may not have a name of her own, a reputation of her own—what does it signify? John, the son of Emily Sandford!—oh no, that was not his natural description. He was John, the son of Robert May. And Robert May was the convict whom he had picked up in the street, of whom he had been so kindly indulgent, so contemptuously tolerant.

John did not follow this train of thought. It gleamed before him as he went along, that was all; and once more he paused on the middle of the bridge, remembering how he had done so before at the different crises of his life. How he had smiled not so many days ago, on his birthday, when he passed over it and thought of his own boyish despair at seventeen, and the impulse he had felt to rush away, and cut all the ties that bound him, and go off to the ends of the world to struggle out a career for himself all alone. At twenty-one he had looked out over the same parapet, on what seemed the same outgoing sails, and had laughed to himself in high self-complacence and content at that foolish petulance of his youth. It was not yet three weeks ago—but then he had felt himself the master of his own fate with prosperity and hope in every circumstance of his life—the ball at his foot as he had said. Not three weeks ago! and now here he stood a ruined man, crushed by disgrace and humiliation, and made to appear as if in his own person he deserved that doom—the son of his father!—doing what he had always been expected to do, betraying those who trusted in him. John grasped the stony parapet and looked—oh no, with no idea of self-destruction—that was an impossible as it was a contemptible mode of escape: but with a bitter indignant persuasion that his early plan would have been the best, and that to have gone away beyond the knowledge of any who had ever heard his name—away into the unknown, fatherless, motherless, friendless—would have been after all the most expedient for him, the only wise thing to do.

A convict: a convict! He went on afterwards setting his teeth, saying this to himself. It was not a thing that could be thought over calmly: his thinkings got into mere repetition to himself of these words, which seemed to circle about him like the flies in the air as he walked on. A convict! There was not the slightest reason to doubt it: it proved itself: no man but one could have held in his imagination and recollection that old innocent picture which had been John's so long. The pretty innocent little picture that might have come out of a child's book, with its little spice of innocent wrongness, the baby disorder, the mutinous pleasure of it! It had been sweet to his memory for years—and now all at once it became horrible, a thing his heart grew sick to think of.

John felt that to few people could it be so horrible as it was to him. Honour and integrity, and noble meaning, and a high scorn of everything base had been the very air he breathed. He had stood on this foundation as some people stand on wealth, and some on family and connections. The other pupils in the office had in many cases possessed a foundation of that other kind: but, as for John, he had always stood high on those personal qualities, on the fact that no reproach could be brought against him, and that whatever records were brought to light he never could be shamed.

That very morning when he set out to go to the office, puzzled about the loss of the copy, but fearing nothing, feeling in all heaven and earth no shadow of anything to fear, with his papers in his pocket, there was not so much as that cloud like a man's hand to warn him. And yet he had been on the eve of irremediable and ruinous disgrace. Only to think of it—this morning with a spotless reputation and every prognostic in his favour: and now—a convict's son!

When the soul is overcome in this way with sudden trouble, how constantly does the sufferer feel that the blow has been administered skilfully in that way of all others which cuts most deeply. There were many other kinds of suffering which John could have borne, he thought, patiently enough—but this! Shame! It was the defeat of all his efforts, the keen and poignant contradiction of all he had striven after. And he was wise enough to know that the first impulse of indignant resistance and that cry of despair with which a man protests that he cannot and will not bear what has befallen him—were alike futile. There it was, not to be got over; and bear it he must, whatever ensued.

In this maze of dreadful thought, he came home to the little rooms in which his virtuous and austere young life had been passed, not knowing in the least what he was going to do, feeling only that he must acknowledge the—man—the convict—acknowledge him, and thus give him more or less the command of his life. John had been in a fever of excitement and suspense when he went away. He was now calm enough, quite quiet and resolute, though he had as yet no plan of action. He walked quickly, absorbed in himself and the consequences to himself, without thinking of what might have happened on the other side; not able, indeed, without a sinking sensation, to think of the other side at all—and pushed open the door which was unlatched. Probably he had left it so when he went out, he could not tell. He did not remember indeed anything about how he had come out. Mr. Barrett's appearance and every secondary circumstance had disappeared from his mind; yet he woke, as he felt the door give way under his hand, to the idea that he must have left it so. It is not a thing to do in London, not even in a quiet little street out of the way. Probably he had done it in his madness in the first shock of his dismay.

It gave him an extraordinary check in the height of his concentrated self-control, to find everything empty when he came in. There was no trace even that anyone had ever been there. The respectable little sitting-room looked exactly as it had done ever since he knew it—the chairs put back in their places, the *Standard* carefully folded upon the table where he had left it in the morning, no appearance anywhere that anything had happened since then. He stood still for a moment with a gasp of dismay, wondering whether he had only dreamt all this, if it had been a mere nightmare, a feverish vision. Could he but persuade himself that this was so, that he was the same John Sandford he had been in the morning, with the ball still at his foot! For the moment a wild hope gleamed across him; but it was only for a moment. He sat down and stared about him, wondering to see everything the same. All the same! yet altogether changed, as no external convulsion could have changed it: an earthquake would have been nothing in comparison. If a bomb had suddenly exploded upon the decent carpet among the inoffensive furniture, and shattered the innocent house to pieces, what would that have been in comparison? These were the ridiculous thoughts that came across his mind, and almost made him laugh in the first revulsion of feeling, which was disappointment and relief, and yet was nothing at all. For what did it matter? The thing had been, and could not be wiped out. It existed and could never be swept away. Ignore it if he could, forget it even if he could, there all the same it would be. He could not be rid of it ever, for ever. He sat silent awhile realising this, and then rose and went to ring the bell: but, before he could touch it, he was startled by a tap at the door.

It was only his landlady who came in—but she had her best cap on, and looked as if she had something to say. She was embarrassed, and turned round and round on her finger a ring which was too big for her.

'If you please, Mr. Sandford——' she began.

'Yes? I left two—people here. Do you know where they have gone?'

'That's why I made so bold as to come in, Mr. Sandford. I don't like saying of it, sir. You have always been a gentleman as I've been glad to have in my house.'

'Yes. What message did they leave? Where have they gone? I came back expecting to find them here.'

'I never was fond of young gentlemen,' said Mrs. Short, taking out her handkerchief. 'They pay well, as a rule, and they don't give much trouble, being out all day: but I've always been afraid of them. They're chancy-like— you don't know what they may do, or who they may bring.'

'Another time,' said John, 'if you've anything to say to me—but at present I want to know what message—— Did they say where they were going?'

'The gentlemen said nothing to me, nor to no one. They just scuttled out of the house, leaving all the chairs about. I thank my goodness gracious stars that I can't see nothing gone: but, Mr. Sandford—I've a great respect for you, sir, as a gentleman that can take care of yourself when many can't, and always tidy, and keeps no bad company, leastways never did till now——'

John only half understood what she was saying, but he caught at the words bad company, and replied, with a faint laugh,

'I've been very particular about that, have I not?' he said.

'Yes, sir: to do you justice, you've been very particular. And that makes me feel it all the more. Do you know, Mr. Sandford, who's been out and in of *my* house all these days, sitting in my parlour, like he was the master? Oh, don't tell me, sir, as you knew all the time! A man as has just come out of prison, a man as has just served out his time, and that was fourteen years. Mr. Sandford, don't tell me as you knew!'

'Yes,' said John; 'I knew; but I didn't know——' here he stopped and gazed at her, quieted he could not tell by what sentiment, and feeling as if the words hung suspended in the air which he ought to have said. 'I didn't know he was—my father'—that was what he had intended to say.

'I'm very sorry, sir,' the woman said. 'You've always been most regular, paying to the day, and always civil, and a pleasure to serve you; but I can't do with that sort of visitors in my house. I can't, sir; I've got my character to think of. I've told Betsy, if they come again, to shut the door in their face. And, Mr. Sandford, it's a week's notice, please, sir. I don't doubt but you can easy suit yourself. There are folks that think nothing of their character so long's they get a good let: and except for this I haven't got a word, not a word, to say against you.'

John stared at her blankly, taking her meaning with difficulty into his mind: then gradually perception came to him.

'You want me,' he said, 'to go away?'

'Yes, sir, that's what it's come to,' the woman said, clearing her throat.

John kept his eyes upon her—trying to intimidate her, she thought; in reality, trying to fathom her, to make out what she meant—then he burst into a sudden laugh.

'To go away—for what? Because I am—in trouble, because my life is not so happy as it has been. Well, it is a good reason enough. Yes, Mrs. Short, I'll go.'

'You—in trouble, sir!' The woman's voice rose into a sort of shriek. 'Oh, Mr. Sandford, what have you done? you that were always so respectable. Can't you put it right? Oh, Mr. Sandford, I never thought of that. How much is it? Tell your ma, sir, and, whatever it costs her, she'll set it right.'

John found himself strangely amused by all this. It came into the midst of his misery like a scrap of farce to relieve his strained bosom by laughter. He knew well enough, too, the phraseology and ways of thinking of his landlady, and he tried to understand the idea he had suggested to her imagination; and half to keep up the joke, though it was a poor one, half because he was incapable of explanations, he made no other reply.

'Oh, Mr. Sandford,' she cried again, coming up to him, laying her hand on his arm, 'excuse me if I make too free; but tell your ma, sir, for the love of God. She'll not let you come to shame for a bit of money. Oh, no, no, no! I can tell by myself. I never breathed a word of it to any mortal, but my Tom was once—he was once—I never knew how it could have been, for a better boy never was. It was some temptation of the devil, sir, that's what it was. I saw the boy was miserable, but I couldn't get a word out of him—till at last one night I went down on my knees, and I got hold of him where he was sitting with his head in his hands, and forced it from him. It was a good bit of money, sir. I'll not say but it kept me low a long time: but what was that in comparison with my Tom's credit, and his situation, and his whole life? He would have fled the country next day, if I hadn't got it out of him that night. Now, Mr. Sandford, haven't I a right to speak? Oh, for God's sake, go out before you sleep and tell your ma!'

'Mrs. Short, you are a good woman. It's not what you think. I am not in debt, nor is it money that troubles me. And my mother knows; I've told her. Thank you for speaking. I'll go as soon as I have found another set of rooms, or perhaps I may go abroad. But, anyhow, I'll clear out within the week since you wish it.'

'Your mother knows?' said Mrs. Short, with a tremble in her voice.

'Yes—everything,' said John, with a smile and a sigh.

'And about these—men? If so be as she knows—and you'll promise to see them no more——'

'I can't give any promise,' said John, shaking his head. But he looked her in the face, in a way, Mrs. Short thought, that those who are falling into bad company and evil ways never do. He was not afraid to meet her eye. She shook her head standing over him, feeling that the problem was one which it was above her power to solve. She said at last, in a subdued tone:

'If you've told your ma—she wouldn't countenance what was wrong. Oh, Lord, I wish I knew what to do for the best. Mr. Sandford, if it's really true that your ma knows, I'll take back my warning, sir, and we'll try again. But oh, you're young, and you don't know how quick things go when you take the wrong road. Oh, Mr. Sandford, though you've had so much of your liberty, you're very young still!'

'Do you think so?' said John, with a faint smile. He felt a hundred: there seemed no spring of youth or hope left in him. Then he said suddenly, with an almost childlike appeal to human kindness: 'I've had no food all day. Go and get me something to eat like a kind soul. I've had no dinner or anything.'

'No dinner!' she said, with an outcry of distress. This seemed something so dreadful, such a breach of all natural laws, that it swept away every lesser emotion. And John, too, though he had said this not because he was hungry, felt a little quiver in his own lip as he realised the extraordinary fact. He had had no dinner! Such a thing had perhaps never happened before in his whole life.

In the evening, when he sat alone with no company but his lamp, having eaten and refreshed himself (and to his own great wonder he was quite hungry when food was set before him, though he did not think he could have tasted a morsel), John heard a soft step pass two or three times close to his window. The street was very quiet after dark, and there was so much significance in the persistent re-passing, so close as if the passer-by meant to look in at the sides of his blind, that his attention was roused. He looked out cautiously, but saw no one. His heart began to beat high—who could it be but one person? John recollected suddenly the soft tread, the cautious, carefully-poised foot, as of one used to moving about steadily, to wearing shoes such as indoor dwellers wear. It came over him with a sickening sensation that a tread so soft would be useful to those who lived by preying upon others: and then a bitter self-reproach seized him: for the unfortunate who had suddenly become so interesting to him, was not, he said to himself, after all a common thief that he should think such horrible injurious things of him. While he was watching, listening, he heard all at once a ring at the door. The stealthy visitor had made up his mind at last. John stood waiting, breathless, in a miserable confusion of feeling, not knowing how he was to meet with, how he was to speak to the man who was his father, when the door opened. But it was not May who came in; it was a figure more unexpected, more startling, the tall dark shadow of a veiled woman, who, putting back part of the shade from her face as she entered noiselessly, presented the grave countenance of his mother, disturbed by unusual excitement to John's astonished eyes.

CHAPTER X.

MOTHER AND SON.

MRS. SANDFORD looked round upon the tidy little sitting-room, but with eyes of alarm that sought in the curtains and shadows for some apparition she feared, and not as a woman looks at the dwelling-place of her child. She had never been here before. Susie had visited him from time to time with a woman's interest in his surroundings, but his mother never. It was all strange to her as if he had been a stranger. She gave that keen look round which noted nothing except what was its object, that there was nobody to be seen.

'Is he here?' she said, in a low voice of alarm, without any greeting or preface. Caresses did not pass between these two either at meeting or at parting, and there was no time to think even of the conventional salutation now.

'No, he is not here.'

She sat down with a sigh of relief, and put back altogether the heavy gauze veil which had enveloped her head.

'Is he coming back? Are you—— Tell them to admit no one, no one! while I am here.'

'I do not think you need fear; he is not coming back.'

She leaned back in her chair with relief. It was the same chair in which *the other* had been sitting when John had left the room in the afternoon. This recollection gave him a curious sensation, as if two images, which were so antagonistic had met and blended in spite of themselves.

'I don't know what I said to you this afternoon; I was so taken by surprise: and yet I was not surprised. I—expected it: only not that it should have happened to you. It is better,' she continued, after a pause, 'that it should have happened to you.'

'Perhaps,' said John; 'I may be better able to bear it—but why did I have no warning that such a thing could be.'

'Oh, why?' said she, with a quick breath of impatience—rather as demanding why he should ask than as allowing the possibility of giving an explanation. She loosened her long black cloak and put it back from her shoulders, and thus the shadows seemed to open a little, and the light to concentrate in her pale, clear face. It is but rarely, perhaps, that children observe the beauty of their mothers, and never, save when it is indicated to them by the general voice, or by special admiration. John had never thought of Mrs. Sandford in this light; but now it suddenly struck him for the first time that she had been, that she was, a woman remarkable in appearance, as in character, with features which she had not transmitted to her children, no common-place, comely type, but features which seemed meant for lofty emotions, for the tragic and impassioned. She had not been in circumstances, so far as he had seen her, to develop these, and her lofty looks had fallen into rigidity, and the austereness of rule and routine. Sometimes they had melted when she looked at Susie, but no higher aspect than that of a momentary softening had ever animated her countenance in his ken. Now it was different. Her fine nostrils moved, dilating and trembling, with a sensitiveness which was a revelation to her son; her eyes shone; her mouth, which was so much more delicate than he had been aware, closed with an impassioned force, in which, however, there was the same suspicion of a quiver. Her face was full of sensation, of feeling, of passion. She was not the same woman as that austere and authoritative one whom he had all this time known. When he returned from giving the order which she asked, that nobody should be admitted, he found her leaning back in her chair with her eyes closed, which seemed to make the rest of her face, which was all quivering with emotion, even more expressive than before.

'I thought that I had not told you enough—that you deserved explanations, which, painful, most painful as they are, ought to be given to you now. I suppose I told you very little to-day?'

'Nothing, or next to nothing,' he replied.

'I suppose—I wanted to spare myself,' she said, with a faint quiver of a smile.

'Mother,' cried John, 'I will take it for granted. Why should you make yourself wretched on my account? And, after all, when the fact is once allowed, what does it matter? I know all that I need to know—now.'

'Perhaps you are right, John. You know what I would have died to keep from your knowledge, if it were not folly and nonsense to use such words. Much, much would be spared in this world if one could purchase the extinction of it by dying. I know that very well: it is a mere phrase.'

He made no reply, but watched with increasing interest the changes in her face.

'It was thought better you should not know. What good could it have done you? A father dead is safe; he seems something sacred, whatever he may have been in reality. *I* thought, I don't shrink from the responsibility, that it was better for you; and my father agreed with me, John.'

'Grandmother did not,' he said, quickly; 'now I know what she meant.'

'Then,' she said, 'now that you know, you can judge between us.'

She made no appeal to his affection. She was not of that kind. And John was sufficiently like her to pause, not to utter the words that came to his lips. He seemed once more to see himself in his boyhood, so full of ambition and pride and confidence. After awhile he said,

'It is much for me to say, but I think I approve. If it is hard upon me as a man, what would it have been when I was a boy?'

'I am glad,' she said, 'that you see it in that light;' and then she paused, as if concluding that part of the subject. She resumed again, after a moment: 'I took every precaution. We disappeared from the place, and changed our name. My father and mother changed their home, broke the thread—I left no clue that I could think of.' She stopped again and cleared her throat, and said, with difficulty, 'Does he think he has any clue?'

John could not make any reply. How his heart veered from side to side!—sometimes all with her in her pride and passion, sometimes touched with a sudden softening recollection of the man with his sophistries, his self-reconciliating philosophy, his good humour, and his almost childish, ingratiating smile.

'I don't see how he can have found out anything. I have never lost sight of him—that was easy enough. He has had whatever indulgences, or alleviations of his lot were permitted. I left money in the chaplain's hand for him when the time came for his coming out. I did not trust the chaplain even with any clue.'

The balance came round again as she spoke, and John remembered how, in this very room, the same story had been told to him from the other side, and he had himself cried out, indignantly, 'Could you not find them? Was there no clue?'

He said now, breathlessly, 'Did you think that right?'

'Right!' She paused with a little gasp, as if she had been stopped suddenly in her progress by an unexpected touch. 'Could there be any question on the subject?'

'Did Susie think it right?'

'Susie!' She paused again with impatience. 'Susie is one of those women who are all-forgiving, and who have no judgment of right and wrong.'

'And you never hesitated, mother!'

'Never,' she said, a faint colour like the reflection of a flame passing over her pale face. 'Why should I hesitate? Could there be a question? Alas! Fate has done it instead of me: but could I—I, your mother, bring such a wrong upon you of my own free will? Don't you think I would rather have died—to use that foolish phrase again—I use it to mean the extremity of wish and effort,—rather than have exposed you to know, much less to encounter—? Don't let us speak of it,' she said, giving her head a slight nervous shake, as if to shake the thought far from her. 'Upon that subject I never had a doubt.'

'And yet he was a man, like other men: and his children at least were not his judges. Most men who have children have something, somebody to meet them after years of separation.'

'Did he say that?'

'He did not blame anybody. Knowing nothing about it but that he was a wretched poor criminal, and that this was his story, I, who was one of the offenders without knowing, was very indignant.'

'You were very indignant!'

'Yes, mother; I thought it cruel. My heart ached for the man; fourteen years of privation and loneliness, and not a soul to say "Welcome" when he came back into the cold world.'

'He had money, which buys friends—the kind of friends he liked.'

She had changed her attitude, and sat straight up, her eyes shining, the lines of her face all moving, rising up enraged and splendid in her own defence.

'It seemed to have gone to his heart—the abandonment—and it went to mine, merely to hear the story told.'

'I bow,' she said, 'to the tenderness of both your hearts! I always felt there was a certain likeness. I act on other laws:—to bring a convict back into my family, to shame my young, high-minded, honourable son, whose path in life promised no difficulty; to shame my gentle child who has all a woman's devotion to whoever suffers or seems to suffer; I don't speak of myself. For myself, I would die a hundred times (that phrase again!) rather than be exposed—— No, no, no—nothing, nothing would have induced me to act otherwise. You don't know what it is—you don't know what *he* is.

- 65 -

Fate, I will not say God, has baffled my plans: but do not let him come near me, for I cannot bear it. I will rather leave everything and go away—to the end of the world.'

John had in his heart suffered all that a proud and pure-minded young man can suffer from the thought of what and who his father was: and he had felt his heart sicken with disgust, turning from him and loathing him. But when his mother spoke thus a sudden revulsion of feeling arose in him. He could not hear him so assailed. A sudden partisanship, that family solidarity which is so curious in its operations, filled his mind. He felt angry with her that she attacked him, though she said no more than it had been in his own heart to say.

He replied, with some indignation in the calmness of his words:

'I think you may save yourself trouble on that account. I have not seen him again. When I came back he was gone. They had not waited for me. They left no message. I don't know where to find him.'

'Gone?' she said. 'Gone——?'

'Yes, mother. He delivered me from the difficulty, the misery in which I was coming back, with the intention of saying—what it is so hard to say to a man who—may be one's—father.' John grew pale, and then grew red. The word was almost impossible to utter, but he brought it forth at last. 'But he did not wait for my hesitation or difficulties. He relieved me. They were gone without leaving a sign.'

'Who do you mean by they?'

'He had a friend,' John answered, faltering, 'a friend who is my friend too. An actor, Montressor.'

'Montressor!' said Mrs. Sandford, with something like a scream. Then she covered her eyes suddenly with her hand. 'Oh, what scenes, what scenes that name brings back to me! they were friends, as such men call friendship. They encouraged each other in all kinds of evil. Montressor! and how came he to be a friend of yours?'

'It is an old story, mother: I daresay you have forgotten. It was entirely by chance. Susie knows. I will make a confession to you,' he said, with a sudden impulse. 'I was very unhappy, and full of resentment towards everybody——'

'Towards me,' she said, quietly, 'I remember very well. That was the time when you said I was Emily, and would not have me for your mother.'

She smiled at the boyish petulance, as a mother thus outraged has a right to smile: and perhaps it was natural she should remember it so. But it was not the moment to remind him. He smiled too, but his smile was not of an easy kind.

'I was altogether wrong,' he said, 'I confess it. When I met this man, I called myself—by the name which seemed to come uppermost in that whirl of trouble. I said I was John May.'

She was silent for a time, not making any reply, her anger not increased, as he thought it would be: for, indeed, her mind was too full to be affected by things which at ordinary times would have moved her much.

'And so,' she said, after a time, 'that was how he found you out. I will not call it fate—it seems like God. And yet, for such a childish, small offence, it was a dreadful penalty. Poor boy! you thought to revenge yourself a little more on me—and instead you have brought upon your own head—this——'

In the silence that followed—for what could John reply?—there came a slight intrusion of sound from the house. Some one went out or came in downstairs, a simple sound, such as in the natural state of affairs would not even have roused any attention. It awakened all the smouldering panic in Mrs. Sandford's face. She started, and caught John by the arm.

'What's that? What's that? It is some one coming—he is coming back.'

'No, mother. It is the people below.'

'Where is he?' she cried, huskily, recovering herself, yet not loosing John's arm. 'Where is he? Where does he live?—not here, don't say he is here.'

'I don't know where he lives. He has never told me, and he left no message, no address.'

'No address,' she said. 'You don't know where he lives, to stop him, but he knows where you live, to hold you in his power. I will meet him in the face when I go out from your door.'

The horror in her looks was so great that John tried to soothe her.

'There is no reason to fear that. He went away, though I had asked them to wait. Perhaps he will come no more.'

'Do me one favour, John,' she cried, grasping his arm closer; 'do this one thing for me. Before he can come home again, before he can find you out, this very night, if you are safe so long, leave this place. Find somewhere else to live in. Oh! you shall have no trouble. I will find you a place; but leave this, leave it now at once. Leave him no clue. What? he has left you none, you say? Why should you hesitate? Come away with me, John. For the love of God! and if you have learned to feel any respect or any pity for your mother—for the poor woman whom once you called Emily—— John, think what it was to me that you should call me Emily, that you should refuse me the name of mother. And yet you were my boy, for whom I had denied myself that you might take no harm. Oh, if you have anything to make up to me for that, do it now. Come away with me to-night, leave this place, let him find no clue, no clue!'

Something of this was said almost in dumb show, her voice giving way in her passion of entreaty. She had clasped his arm in both her hands as her excitement grew. Her breath was hot on John's cheek. There was something in the clasp of her hands, in the force of her passionate determination, that made him feel like a child in her hold.

'Mother,' he said, 'what would be the use? Do you think I could disappear? If ever that was possible, it isn't now. Whoever wants to find me, if not here, will find me at the office, or wherever I may be working. I can't sink down through a trap-door into the unknown; that might be on the stage but not in real life. How could one like me, with work to do for my living, and employers and people that know me, disappear?'

A remnant, perhaps, of John's own self-esteem, which had been so bitterly pulled down by the incidents of this day, awoke again. It was only the insignificant who could obliterate themselves and leave no clue. For him to do it was impossible. It was but a melancholy pride, but it was pride still.

'He will not go to the office after you. He knows none of your friends. If you leave this, and give no address, he will perhaps not seek for you, for that would be a great deal of trouble. He never liked trouble. We should gain time at least to think what should be done. John, do what I ask you! Come away with me to-night. I will manage everything. You shall have no trouble. John!'

'Mother,' he cried, taking her hands into his, 'at the end, when all is said that can be said, he is our father, Susie's and mine. We can't leave him alone to perish. We can't forsake him. Mother, now that I know the truth, I know it, and there is an end. I can't put it out of my mind again. I thought my father was dead, but he is not dead, he is alive. It can never be put out of sight again. It may be bitter enough, terrible enough, but we can't put it out of our minds. There it is—he is alive. He is my business more than anything else. There can be no choice for Susie and me.'

She had been trying to free her hands while he spoke. She wrung them out of his hold now, thrusting him from her.

'I might have known,' she said, trembling with anger and misery, 'I might have known! Susie, too. What does it matter that I have protected you, saved you, guarded you? I am not your business, I or my comfort— but he—he—— What will you do with him? where will you take him? If he comes here, the woman of this house will not bear it long, I warn you. What will you do, John? Will you take him to your village among the people you care for? Where will you take him? What will you do with him, John?'

'My village?' John said. And there came over him a chill as of death. His face grew ashy pale, his limbs refused to support him longer; he sank into the vacant chair, and leaned his head, which swam, on his two hands, and looked at his mother opposite to him with eyes wild with sudden dismay and horror: all the day long amid his troubles he had not thought of that. His village! And must he tell this dreadful story there? and unfold all the new revelations of failure, betrayal, disgrace—and of how he had no name, and only shame for an inheritance? Must he tell it all *there*?

CHAPTER XI.

SUSIE AND HER LOVERS.

SUSIE had been nearly a month in Edgeley, and a new faculty had developed in her—a faculty that lies dormant for a life long with many people, and that is impossible to others—the faculty of living in the country. She had never known what that was. Not only in town, in the midst of London, but in the strange, rigid, conventional, severely-regulated life of the great hospital, she had spent all the most important years of her life, and thought she knew no other way. Had she been interrogated on the subject, Susie would have said that the country might be very good for a change—it was, as everybody knew, the very place for convalescents; where people ought to be sent to get well: but for those who were well to start with, oh no! This she would have said in all good faith, in that serene unacquaintance with what she rejected, which is the panoply of the simple mind.

But when she got to the country, almost the first morning Susie woke up in the quiet, in the clear air, and kind, mild sunshine which beamed out of the skies like a smile of God, and had no stony pavement to rebound from and turn into an oven—with a soft rapture such as all her life she had never known before. She had thought she liked the crowd, the stir, the perpetual call upon her, and what people called the life, which was nowhere so vigorous, so intent, so full of change, as in town. But in a moment she became aware that all this was a mistake, and that it was for the country she had been born. This had been a delightful revelation to Susie. And there had followed quickly another revelation, which never is unimportant in a young woman's life, but which in her peculiar existence had been somehow eluded: and this was her own possession of that feminine power and influence of which books are full, but which Susie had not seen much of in ordinary life. Sometimes, indeed, there had happened cases in which a young doctor had somehow been transported beyond the line of his duties, by some one, perhaps a sister, most probably a young lady on probation, or one who was playing at nursing, as some will. And this had been at once wrong, which gave it piquancy as an incident, and amusing. But such incidents were very rare; people in the hospital being too busy to think of anything of the kind. Susie had been, without knowing, the object of one or two dawning enthusiasms of this description. In one case she had perhaps vaguely suspected the possibility: but Mrs. Sandford gave neither opportunity nor encouragement, and the thing had blown over.

Now, however, it had fully dawned upon her that she herself, tranquil and simple in early maturity, no longer a girl, as she said to herself, nor in the age of romance, had come to that moment of sovereignty which sooner or later falls to most women, notwithstanding all statistics—the power of actually affecting, disposing of, the life of another. It does not always turn out to be of profound importance in a man's life that he has been refused by a certain woman. But for the time, at least, both parties feel that it is of great importance: and the result of acceptance, colouring and determining the course of two lives, cannot be exaggerated. Susie discovered, first with amusement, afterwards with a little fright, that the visits of Percy Spencer and of Mr. Cattley were not without meaning. The two curates, who were so different! Their position gave them a certain right to come, and her position as a stranger and a temporary inhabitant exempted her, so far, at least, as she was aware, from the remarks and criticisms to which another young woman living alone might have been subject. But Susie had nobody to interfere, no duenna, not even a well-trained maid to say not at home. These visitors came in with a little preliminary knock at the parlour door without asking if it was permitted—without any formality of announcement. The door of the house was always open, and Sarah in the kitchen would have thought it strange indeed to be interrupted in her morning work by anyone ringing at the bell.

A month is a long time when it is passed in this land of intimacy. Susie was asked frequently to the rectory, not always with Mrs. Egerton's free will—but there are necessities in that way which ladies in the country cannot ignore: and it was very rarely that a day passed without a meeting in the village street, if no more—at some cottage where Susie had made herself useful, but most frequently in her own little sanctuary, in the parlour so familiar to both these gentlemen, so much more familiar to them than to her. At first they were continually meeting there, and their meetings were not pleasant. For Percy did his best to exasperate Mr. Cattley by a pretended deference to his old age and antiquated notions, or by the elevation of his own standard of churchmanship over the mild pretensions of the clergyman who did not call himself a priest. And Mr. Cattley would retaliate by times with a middle-aged contempt for boyish enthusiasms, by assuring his young friend that by-and-by he would see things in a different light.

After a while, however, they fell into a system, arranging their comings and goings with a mutual and jealous care in order that they might not meet. And they both gave Susie a great deal of information about themselves. She sat, and smiled, and listened, not without a subdued pleasure in that power which she had discovered later than usual, and which even this mutual antagonism made more flattering. Percy was full of schemes in which he demanded her interest.

'Everything has gone on here in the old-fashioned way,' he said, 'in the famous old let-alone way. Aunt Mary has pottered about: she is the only one that has done anything. My father never had any energy. He would have let anyone take the reins out of his hands. And she has done it; and she has always had old Cattley under her thumb. He has not dared to say his soul was his own. To see him sit and stare and worship her used to be our fun when we were boys. Jack must have told you.'

'No, never. John saw nothing that was not perfect. He worshipped all of you, I think.'

'Some of us too much, perhaps—not me, I am certain,' said Percy. 'But old Cattley was the greatest joke, Miss Sandford. How you would have laughed!' (Susie, however, did not laugh at all at this suggestion, but sat as grave as a judge, with her eyes bent on her sewing.) 'But nothing could have been more unecclesiastical,' Percy continued, recovering his gravity. 'It was the first thing I had to do in getting the parish into my hands. Aunt Mary had to be put down.'

'Has she been put down?' said Susie, laughing a little in her turn.

'I flatter myself, completely,' said the young man. 'She has learned to keep her own place, which is everything. My father gives no trouble; he sees how things have been neglected, and he is quite willing that I should have it all in my own hands. I hope, especially if I have your help, Miss Sandford, to have the cottage hospital and all the improvements of which we have talked carried out. If I might hope that you would set it going——'

'But would not that be like your aunt's interference over again, with no right at all,' Susie said.

'No one can have any right—save what is given them by the clergy. And you are not my aunt—very different! How I should love to delegate as much as is fit of my authority to you!' He paused a moment, with a sigh and tender look, at which Susie secretly laughed, but outwardly took no notice. Then he added: 'Aunt Mary would have no delegation. She interferes as if she thought she had a right to do it—a pretension not tenable for a moment. But to entrust the woman's part—to find an Ancilla Domini, dear Miss Sandford, in you!'

Mr. Cattley was not so lively as this. He would sit for a long time by the little work-table which had belonged to old Mrs. Sandford, and say very little. He would sometimes relate to Susie something about her grandparents, and talk of the pretty old lady with her white hands.

'They were here when I first came,' he would say. 'I was a little lonely when I came. I was one of the youngest of an immense family. My people were glad to get rid of us, I think, especially the young ones, who were of no great account. And my mother was dead. Edgeley was very pleasant to me. I was taken up at the rectory as if I had been a son of the house. And nobody can tell what she—what they all—were to me.'

Mr. Cattley coughed a little over the *she*, to make it look as if it were a mistake, changing it into *they*.

'Mrs. Egerton,' said Susie, with a directness which brought a little colour to the old curate's cheek, 'must have been very pretty then.'

'To me she is beautiful now,' he said, fervently, 'and always will be. I am not of the opinion that age has anything to do with beauty. It becomes a different kind. It is not a girl's or a young woman's beauty any longer, but it is just as beautiful. You will forgive me, Miss Sandford——'

'I have nothing to forgive,' said Susie, but she said it with a little heat. 'I like people to be faithful,' she added, perhaps indiscreetly.

Mr. Cattley did not answer for some time. And then he said:

'I am going away now, and another life is beginning. I have been rather a dreamer all my life, but I must be so no longer. I begin to feel the difference. I think, if you will not be offended, that it is partly you who have taught me——'

'I!' cried Susie, with something like fright. 'I don't know how that could be——'

'Nor I either,' he said, with a smile which Susie felt to be very ingratiating. 'You have not intended it, nor thought of it, but still you have done it. There is something that is so real in you, if I may say so—a sweet, practical truth that makes other people think.'

'You mean,' said Susie, with a blush, 'that I am very matter-of-fact?'

'No, I don't mean that. I suppose what I mean is, that I have been going on in a kind of a dream, and you are so living that I feel the contrast. You must not ask me to explain. I'm not good at explaining. But I know what I mean. I wish you knew Overton, Miss Sandford.'

'Yes,' said Susie, simply, 'I should like to know it—when do you go?'

He smiled vaguely.

'That is what I can't tell,' he said. 'I should be there now. When do *you* go, Miss Sandford?'

'I don't know that either,' she said, with a blush of which she was greatly ashamed. 'I suppose I ought to go now: but the country life is pleasant, far more than I could have thought, after living so long in town.'

'You have always lived in town?'

'As long as I can remember,' said Susie.

'That is perhaps what makes one feel that you are living through and through. It must quicken the blood. Now I,' said Mr. Cattley, 'am a clodhopper born. I love everything that belongs to the country, and nothing of the town—except——' he said, and laughed and looked at her with pleasant, mild, admiring eyes.

'You must make an exception,' said Susie, 'or you will seem to say that you dislike me.'

He shook his head at that with a smile—as if anything so much out of the question could be imagined by no one. It was all very simple, tranquil, and sweet, nothing that was impassioned in it, perhaps a little too much of the middle-aged composure and calm. But Susie liked the implied trust, the gentle entire admiration and appreciation. It might not be romantic, perhaps, but she had a feeling that she might go to Overton or anywhere putting her hand in that of this mild man. If there was a little prick of feeling in respect to Mrs. Egerton, who had been so long the object of his devotion, that was soothed by the natural triumphant confidence of youth in its own unspeakable superiority over everyone who was old: and to Susie at twenty-six (though that, she was willing to allow, was not very young) a woman of forty-eight was a feminine Methusaleh, and certainly not to be feared.

Nothing more had been said; and these two were tranquilly sitting together; she at her work, he close to her little table, in a pleasant silence which might have been that of the profoundest calm friendship, or the most tranquil domestic love. And it might have ended in nothing more than was then visible—a great mutual confidence and esteem: or it might end at any moment in the few words which would suffice to unite these two lives into one for all their mortal duration. But as they sat there silently, in that intense calm fellowship, the ears of both were caught by the sound of hurried footsteps approaching, so quick, so precipitate, that it was not possible to dissociate them from the idea of calamity.

Mr. Cattley lifted his head and looked towards the door; Susie involuntarily put down her work. She thought of an accident, in the semi-professional habit of her thoughts, and her mind leaped naturally into the question where she could find bandages and the other appliances? while he, whose duty took another turn, instinctively felt in his breast-pocket for the old well-worn Prayer-book, from which he was never separated. Then there was a clang of the open door, pushed against the wall by some one entering eagerly. And the next moment the parlour door burst open, and Elly appeared—Elly with her eyes very wide open and shining, her mouth set firm, a wind of vigorous and rapid movement coming in with her, disturbing the papers on the table. The curate jumped up in alarm, with a cry: 'Elly, what is the matter?' and a changing colour. Susie thought the same as he did—that something must have happened at the rectory, and rose up, but not with the same eagerness as he.

'Oh, you are here, Mr. Cattley,' said Elly, with an impatient wave of her hand. She was breathless, scarcely able to get out the words, which ran off in a sort of sibilation at the end. Then she sat down hastily, and paused to take breath. 'It was Susie,' she went on, with a gasp, 'that I wanted to see.'

'I will go away,' said the curate, 'but tell me first that nothing is wrong—that nothing has happened.'

Elly took a minute or two to recover her breath, which she drew in long inspirations, relieving her heart.

'Since you are here,' she said, 'you may stay, for you have known everything. Nothing wrong? Oh, everything is wrong. But nothing has happened to Aunt Mary, if that is what you mean.'

Mr. Cattley grew very red, and cast a glance at Susie, who on her part sat down quickly, silently, without asking any question, which had its significance. Perhaps she only felt that, as there was evidently no need for bandages she could not have much to do with it, either; perhaps—but it is unnecessary to investigate further. For Elly added, immediately,

'I have got a letter from Jack, which I don't understand at all.'

She had recovered her breath. There was an air of defiance and resolution upon her face. She drew her chair into the open space in front of Susie, and challenged her as if to single combat.

'I want to know,' she said, 'from you—I don't mind Mr. Cattley being there, because he knows us both so well, and has been in it all along. I want to know, from you—is there any reason, any secret reason, that he could find out and did not know before, that could stand between Jack and me?'

Susie looked at her with an astonished face, her mouth a little open, her eyes fixed in wonder. She did not make any reply, but that was comprehensible, for the question seemed to take her altogether by surprise.

'I don't think you understand me,' said Elly, plaintively, 'and I'm sure I don't wonder. *You* know, Mr. Cattley, at least; Jack went away full of his great scheme which was to make him rich, which was to make Aunt Mary's opposition as much contrary to prudence as it was to—to good sense and—everything,' cried Elly, 'for of course the only drawback in it, as everybody must have seen with half an eye, was that I was not good enough for him, a rising engineer, with the finest profession in the world! However, we were engaged all the same. People might say not, but we were—in every sense of the word—I to him and he to me!'

Her face was like the sky as she told her tale, now swept by clouds, now clearing into full and open light. She grew red and pale, and dark and bright in a continued succession, and kept her eyes fixed with mingled defiance and appeal on Susie's face.

'Now tell me,' she said, 'for you must know—is there anything that Jack could find out that would change all that in a moment? What is there that he could find out that would make him think differently of himself and of every creature? Can't you tell me, Susie? You are his only sister; you must know, if anyone knows. What is it? What is it? Mr. Cattley, her face is changing too. Oh, for goodness sake, make her tell me! If I only knew, I could judge for myself. Make her say what it is!'

The clouds that came and went on Elly's face seemed suddenly to have blown upon that wind of emotion to Susie's. After her first look of wonder, she had given the questioner a quick suspicious troubled glance. Then Susie picked up her work again and bent her head over it, and appeared to withdraw her attention altogether. She went on working in an agitated way a minute or two after this appeal had been made to her. Then she suddenly raised her head.

'What could he have found out? How should I know what he could find out? What was there to find out?'

'These are the questions I am asking you,' cried Elly. 'Here is his letter. I brought it to show you. It is a letter,' cried the girl, 'which anybody may see, not what anyone could call a love-letter. I suppose he has found out, after having spoken, that he did not—care for me as he thought.'

'Elly,' said the curate, 'I know nothing about it—but I am sure *that* is not true.'

'Oh, you should see the letter,' she cried, with a faint laugh. The clouds with a crimson tinge had wrapped her face in gloom and shame. Then she paused and put her hands to her eyes to hide the quick-coming tears. 'Why should one be ashamed?' she said. 'I was not ashamed before. It was I who insisted before; for I was quite sure—quite sure—— And now what am I to think? for he has given me up, Susie, he has given me up!'

Susie kept her head bent over her work.

'Because,' she said, 'of something he has found out?'

'Because of—yes—yes. Read it, if you like—anyone may read it. Because he thought his father was dead and he finds out now that he is alive; but what is his father to me? No father can make a slave of Jack, for he is a man. What have I do with his father, Susie?'

Susie's work served her no longer as a shield. It dropped from her hands: she was very pale, everything swam before her eyes.

'Oh, what is it—what is it—*what is it*?' cried Elly, clapping her hands together with a frenzy of eagerness and anxiety and curiosity, which resounded through the silence of the house.

CHAPTER XII.

JOHN'S LETTER.

THE letter which had been received that morning, and had thrown the rectory into the deepest dismay ran thus:

'DEAREST ELLY,

'After all that we have said and hoped, I am obliged to come to a pause. What I have to tell you had better be said in a very few words. I have always believed that my father was dead, that he died when I was a child. I have suddenly found that he is alive. His existence makes an end at once of all the hopes that were as my life. I must give you up, first of all, because you are more precious than everything else. Whatever may happen to me; whatever I do; whether I succeed, as is very little likely, or fail, which is almost sure now, I never can have any standing-ground on which to claim you. I must give you up. This revolution in my life has been very sudden, and I dare not delay telling you of it—for nothing can ever bridge over the chasm thus made. I will explain why this is, if you wish it, or if anyone wishes it: but I would rather not do it, for it is very, very painful. All is pain and misery—I think there is nothing else left in the world. Elly, I daren't say a word to you to rouse your pity. I ought not to try to make you sorry for me. I ought to do nothing more than say God bless you. I never was worthy to stand beside you, to entertain such a wild dream as that you might be mine. I can never forget, but I hope that you may forget, all except our childhood, which cannot harm.

'J. M. S.'

'Now what,' said Elly, facing them both defiantly, 'what does that mean?'

Susie had read it too, at last, though at first she had refused to read it. Did she not know in a moment what it meant? For her there could be no doubt. Since she had grown a woman; since she had learned how things go in this world, and how difficult it is to conceal anything, there had always been a dread in Susie's mind of what would happen when John found out. This had only come over her by moments, but now, in the shock of the discovery, she believed that she had always thought so, and always trembled for this contingency. She said to herself now that she had always known it would happen, which was going further still—always known—always dreaded—and now it had come. She did not need to read the letter, but she had done so at last, overwhelmed by anxiety and fear. She gave it back to Elly without a word. Of course she had known what it must be. Of course, from the first moment, she had known.

'Susie,' Elly said again, 'tell me, what does it mean?'

'You know him well enough,' Susie said, falteringly; 'you know he would not say what was not true.'

'But if this is true,' said Elly, 'then he has said before what was not true. What can it be to me that his father is living? I do not mind—his father is nothing to me. I don't want to hurt you, Susie, but if his father swept the streets, if he—oh, I don't want to hurt you!'

'You don't hurt me,' said Susie, with the smile of a martyr. 'Oh, Miss Spencer, let us leave it alone. You see what he says. He will explain, if you insist, but he would rather not explain. Don't you trust him enough for that?'

'Trust him!' said Elly. 'I trust him so much that, if he sent me word to go to him and marry him to-morrow, I would do it. I trust him so that I don't believe it, oh, not a word,' the girl cried. And then she threw herself upon Susie, clasping her wrists as she tried, trembling, to resume her work. 'Oh, tell me, what does he mean—what does he mean? What can his father be to me?'

'Elly,' said Mr. Cattley, 'don't you see how hard you are upon her? Take what Jack says, or let him explain for himself. I will go to him and get his explanation, if you wish—but why torture *her*?'

Elly shot a vivid glance from the curate to Susie, who sat with her head bent over her work, her needle stumbling wildly in her trembling hands.

'You think a great deal of sparing her, Mr. Cattley. Aunt Mary says——'

Elly was in so great distress, so excited, so crossed and thwarted, so uncertain and unhappy, that to wound some one else was almost a relief to her. But she stopped short before she shot her dart.

'I am sure she says nothing that is unkind,' said the curate, firmly; but his very firmness betrayed the sense of a doubt. Mrs. Egerton had been his idol all this time, and was he going to desert her? Could she by any possibility think that he was deserting her? His own mind was too much confused and troubled on his own account to be clear.

Susie kept on working as if for life and death, not meeting the girl's look, tacitly resisting the clasp of her hands, grateful when Mr. Cattley distracted Elly's attention and relieved herself from that urgent appeal, yet scarcely conscious whence the relief came or what they were saying to each other to make that pause. Her needle flew along wildly all the time, piercing her fingers more often than the two edges which she was sewing together: and in her mind such a tumult and conflict, half physical from the flutter of her heart beating in her ears, making a whirr of sound through which the voices came vaguely, carrying no meaning. Elly's appeal to her, though so urgent, was but secondary. The thing that had happened, and all the questions involved in it: how he had come to light again, that poor father whom Susie had been brought up to fear, yet whom she could not help loving in a way; how John had found out the family tragedy; what it would be to her mother to be brought face to face with it again, and to know that *he* knew it, whom it had been the object of her life to keep in ignorance. To think that all this had happened, and nobody had told her; that she had not known a word of it till now, when that intimation was accompanied by this impassioned appeal for explanation. Explanation! how could Susie explain? The very suggestion that another mode of treatment was possible from that which her mother had adopted, and that, instead of concealing it at any risk, John was setting it up between him and those he loved most, identifying himself with it, even offering explanation if necessary, was appalling to Susie.

It was only when she had a moment of silence to consider, that it all came upon her. She did not know what they were saying, or desire to hear. She felt by instinct that some other subject had been momentarily introduced, and was grateful for the moment's relief to think. But how could she think in the shock of this unexpected revelation, and with all that noise and singing in her ears? She came to herself a little when the voices ceased, and she became aware that they were looking at her, and wondering why she did not say anything—which was giving up her own cause as much as if she confirmed the truth. She looked up with eyes that were dim and dazed, but tried to smile.

'I cannot tell you what John means,' she said; 'how could I, when I don't know what he means? He has—very high notions: and he thinks—nothing good enough for you. We have no—pretensions—as a family.'

Susie tried very hard to smile and look as if John were only very scrupulous, humble-minded, feeling himself not Elly's equal in point of birth.

'We've gone over all that,' cried Elly, with an impatient wave of her hand. 'And what does it matter—to anybody, now-a-days? It is all exploded; it is all antiquated. Nobody thinks of such a thing now. And Jack knows well enough. Besides, it is ridiculous,' cried the girl; 'he is—well, if you must have it, he is conceited, he is proud of himself, he is no more humble about it than if he were a king. Do you think I'm a fool not to know his faults? I've known them all my life. I like his faults!' Elly said.

And then there was again a pause. Nobody spoke. It became very apparent to both these anxious questioners—to Elly, when the fumes of her own eager speech died away, and to Mr. Cattley, who was calmer—that Susie did not wish to make any reply, that she knew something of which this was the natural consequence, something which she was determined not to tell, something which was serious enough to justify John's letter, which showed that it was no fantastic notion on his part, but a reality. Susie herself was dimly aware, even though she had her eyes on her work as before, that they were looking at her with keen examination, and also in her mind that they were coming to this inevitable conclusion: but what could she do?

'Every family,' she said, faltering, 'has its little secrets, or at least something it keeps to itself. I don't know that there is more with us than with other people——' But her voice would not keep steady. 'The only thing,' she went on, sharply, feeling a resource in a little anger, 'is that people generally—keep these things to themselves;—but John, it seems that John——' And here she came to a dead stop and said no more.

Elly had grown graver and graver while Susie spoke. Her excitement and impatience to know, fell still, as a lively breeze will sometimes do in a moment. Her eyes, which Susie could not meet, seemed to read the very outline of the drooping figure, the bent head, the nervous stumbling hands so busy with work which they were incapable of doing. Elly's face settled into something very serious. She flung her head back with the air of one taking a definite resolution.

'In that case,' she said, lingering a little over the words in case they might call forth an answer, 'in that case, I think I had better go.'

Mr. Cattley, much perplexed, went with her to the door. He went up the street with her, his face very grave too, almost solemn.

'Don't do anything rash, Elly,' he said. 'We know Jack. I—I can't think he is to blame.'

'To blame!' Elly said, with her head high, as if the suggestion were an insult. Then she added, after a moment, 'Yes, he's to blame, as everybody is that makes a mystery. Whatever it is, he might have known that he could trust me; that is the only way in which he can be to blame.'

Susie had thrown away her work in the ease of being alone. It was an ease to her, and the only solace possible. She put her arms on the table and her face upon them, and found the relief which women get in tears. It is but a poor relief; yet it gives a sort of refreshment. Her burning and scorched eyelids were softened—and the sense of scrutiny removed, and freedom to look and cry as she would, was good. But the thronging thoughts that had been kept in check by that need of keeping a steady front to the world, which is at once an appalling necessity and a support to women, came now with a wilder rush and took possession altogether of her being. How was it that he had appeared again, that spectre whom she had feared since she was a child, yet for whom by moments nature had cried out in her heart, Papa! She, like John, only knew the child's name for him, only remembered him as smiling and kind; though she had learned, as John never had learned, that other aspect of him which appeared through her mother's eyes. Susie knew something, embittered by the feeling of the woman who had gone through it all, of the long and hopeless struggle that had filled all her own childhood, and of which she had been vaguely conscious—the struggle between a woman of severe virtue, and an uprightness almost rigid, and a man who had no moral fibre, yet so many engaging qualities, so much good humour, ease of mind, and power of adapting himself, that most people liked him, though no one approved of him: the kind of father whom little children adore, but whom his sons and daughters, as they grow up, sometimes get to loathe in his incapacity for anything serious, for any self-restraint or self-respect.

His wife had been the last woman in the world to strive with such a nature, and perhaps the horror that had grown in her, and which she had instilled unconsciously into Susie's mind, was embittered by this knowledge. Susie knew all the terrible story. How the woman had toiled to keep him right, to convince him of the necessity of keeping right, to persuade him that there was a difference between right and wrong: and she knew that this always hopeless struggle had ended in the misery and horror of the shame which her proud mother had to bear, yet would not bear. All this came back to her as she lay with her head bowed upon her arms in the abandonment of a misery which no stranger's eye could spy upon. And he had come back? and how was mother to bear it? And how had John found it out? And why did he not hide in his own heart, as they had done, this dreadful, miserable secret? She, a girl, had known it and kept it a secret, even from her own thoughts, for fourteen years. Day and night she had prayed for the unfortunate in prison, but never by look or word betrayed the thing which had changed her life at twelve years old, and sundered her from others of her age, more or less completely ever since. It had separated her so completely that till now Susie had never lived in entirely natural easy relations with other girls, or with men of her own age. There had always been a great gulf fixed between her and youthful friendship, between her and love. This had been somehow bridged over here in this innocent place—and now! Oh, how would mother bear it? Oh, how had John found it out?

She was in the midst of these confused yet too distinct and certain trains of recollections and questions, when her solitude and ease of self-abandonment were suddenly disturbed. She had not heard any step, any token of another's presence until she suddenly felt a light touch upon her bowed head, and on her arm. Susie had given herself up too completely to her own thoughts to be capable of considering the plight in which she was. She started and looked up, her face all wet with her weeping. She thought, she knew not what—that it was he perhaps, the terror of the family, though she remembered nothing of him but kindness; or John, it might be John, come to fetch her, to claim her help in these renewed and overwhelming troubles. She started up in haste, raising to the new-comer her tell-tale face. But it was not John, nor her father. It was Mr. Cattley who was standing close by her with his hand touching her arm. He had touched her head before, as she lay bowed down and overwhelmed. His eyes were fixed upon her, waiting till she should look at him, full of pity and tenderness.

'Oh, Mr. Cattley!' she cried, in the extremity of her surprise. He only replied by patting softly the arm on which his hand lay.

'Tell me,' he said, 'what is wrong. Tell me what is wrong. The secret, if it is a secret, will be safe with me: but you cannot bear this pressure; you must have some relief to your mind. Susie—I will call you what Elly calls you for once—do you know what I was going to say to you when she came?'

Susie raised her tear-stained face to his with a little surprise, and said no.

'So much the worse for my chances,' he said, with a faint smile. 'You might have divined, perhaps; yet why should you? I was going to tell you a great many things I will not say now—to explain——' Something like a blush came upon his middle-aged countenance. 'This is not the time for that. I was going to ask you if you would marry me. There: that is all. You see by this that I am ready to keep all your secrets, and help you and serve you every way I can. It is only for this reason that I tell you now. Will you take the good of me, Susie, without troubling yourself with the thought of anything I may ask in return? There, now! Poor child, you are worn out. Tell me what it is.'

'Oh, Mr. Cattley,' she cried, and could say no more.

'Never mind Mr. Cattley: tell me what troubles you—that is the first thing to think of. I guess as much as that it is something which poor Jack has found out, but which you knew. I will go further, and tell you what I guessed long ago—that this poor father has done something in which there was trouble and shame.'

He had seated himself by her and taken her hand, holding it firmly between his, and looking into her face. Susie felt, as many have felt before her, that here all at once was a stranger to whom she could say what she could not have said to the most familiar friend.

'We hoped,' she said, in a low voice—'we thought—that nobody knew.'

'Not John?'

'Oh, John last of all; that was why he lived here; that was why we left him, mother and I, and never came, and let him think that he was nothing to us. He thought we had no love for him. He said to mother once that she was not his mother. Ah!' cried Susie, with a low cry of pain at that recollection, 'all that he might never know.'

'And now he has found out: how do you think he can have found out?'

Susie shook her head.

'The time was up; we knew that, and we were frightened, mother and I, though there seemed no reason for fear, for we had left no sign to find us by. Oh, I am afraid—I was always afraid—that to do that was unkind. He was papa after all; he had a right to know, at least; but mother could not forget all the dangers, all that she had gone through.'

'I suppose, then,' said Mr. Cattley, with a little pressure of her hand, 'his name was not your name?'

Susie looked at him with something like terror. Her voice sank to the lowest audible tone.

'His name—our real name—is May.'

The curate had great command of himself, and was on his guard; nevertheless she felt a thrill in the hand that held hers: Susie sensitive, and prepared to suffer, as are the unfortunate, attempted to draw hers away—but he held it fast; and when he spoke, which was not for a minute, he said, with a movement of his head,

'I think I remember now.'

The grave look, the assenting nod, the tone were all too much for her excited nerves. She drew her hand out of his violently.

'Then if you remember,' cried Susie, 'you know that it was disgrace no one could shake off. You know it was shame to bow us to the dust; that we never could hold up our heads, nor take our place with honest people, nor be friends, nor love, nor marry, with such a weight upon us as that; and now you know why John, poor John, oh, poor John!'

She hurried away from the table where the curate sat, regarding her with that compassionate look, and threw herself into her grandfather's chair which stood dutifully by the side of the blank fireplace where Elly and John had placed it. Her simple open countenance, which had hid that secret beneath all the natural candour and truth of a character which was serene as the day, was flushed with trouble and misery. Life seemed to have revealed its sweeter mysteries to Susie only to show her how far apart she must keep herself from honest people, as she said. And her heart cried out—almost for the first time on its own account. Her thoughts had chimed in with her mother's miseries, but had not felt them, save sympathetically; now her own time had come—and John's—John's, who knew nothing, who must have discovered everything at one stroke; he who was not humble, nor diffident, but so certain of himself and all that he could do. What did it matter for anybody in comparison with John?

Mr. Cattley did not disturb her for some time. He let that passion wear itself out. Then he went and stood with his back to the fireplace, as Englishmen use, though it was empty.

'And now,' he said, 'that we understand, let us lay our heads together and think what can be done.'

'There is nothing to be done,' said Susie. 'Oh, Mr. Cattley, go away, don't pity me. I can't bear it. There is only one thing for me to do, and that is to go home to mother and John.'

'I do not pity you,' he said, 'far from that. You have got the same work as the angels have. Why should I pity you? It hurts them too, perhaps, if they are as fair spirits as we think. But I am going with you, Susie: for two, even when the second is not good for much, are better than one.'

She clasped her hands and looked up at him with a gaze of entreaty.

'Don't,' she cried, 'don't mix yourself up with us! Oh, go away to the people who are fond of you, to the people who are your equals. What has a clergyman to do with a man who has been in prison? Oh, never mind me, Mr. Cattley. I am going to my own belongings. We must all put up with it together the best way we can.'

'Susie,' he said, softly, 'you are losing time. Don't you know there is an evening train?'

CHAPTER XIII.

THE DARKNESS THAT COULD BE FELT.

JOHN rose late next morning to a changed world. It no longer seemed to be of any importance what he did. For the first time in his life he got up in the forenoon and breakfasted as late as if he had been a fashionable young man with nothing to do. He was not fashionable indeed, but there was no longer any occupation that claimed him. He had nothing to do. He flung himself on his sofa, after the breakfast, which he had no heart to touch, had been taken away. What did it matter what he did now? He had not slept till morning. He was fagged and jaded, as if he had been travelling all night. Travelling all night! that was nothing, not worth a thought. How often had he stepped out of a train, and, after his bath and his breakfast, rushed off to the office with his report of what he had been doing, as fresh as if he had passed the night in the most comfortable of beds! that was nothing. Very, very different was it to lie all night tossing, with a fever swarm of intolerable thoughts going through and through your head, and to rise up to feel yourself without employment or vocation, to see the world indifferently swinging on without you, when you yourself perhaps had thought that some one train of things, at least, would come to a dead stand without you. But there was no stoppage visible anywhere. It was he who had stopped like a watch that has run down, but everything else went on as before.

He had written his letter to Elly on the previous night. Thus everything was crammed into one day—his bad reception at the office, his discovery of the man who had thus injured him, who had injured him so much more sorely by the mere fact of existing; and the conclusion of his early romance and love-dream. He had not sent the letter yet. He had kept it open to read it in the morning, to see whether anything should be added or taken away. So many words rose to his lips which appealed involuntarily to Elly's love, to her sympathy—and he did not want to do that. He wanted to be quite imperative about it, as a thing on which there could be no second word to say. Elly could not call a convict father. She must never even know of the man who was John's destroyer, though he was at the same time John's father. He shuddered at the words, notwithstanding that a great melting and softening was in his heart towards the strange, loosely-knitted intelligence which seemed to drift through everything—life, and morality, and natural affection—without feeling any one influence stronger than the other, or any moral necessity, either logical or practical. To be brought thus in all the absolutism of youth, and in all the rigid rightness of young respectability, face to face with a man to whom nothing was absolute, and the most fundamental principles were matters of argument and opinion, gave such a shock to John's being as it is impossible to estimate. It seemed to cut him adrift from everything that kept him to his place. Had the discovery been uncomplicated by anything at the office, John might have felt it differently. It would, in any way, have taken the heart out of him, but it would not, perhaps, have interfered with his work. But now everything was gone.

He flung himself down on the sofa, and lay like a man dead or disabled; like a man, he said to himself, who had been drunk overnight, who had come out of dissipation and vice with eyes that sickened at the light of day. And this was John Sandford, who never in his life before, having unbroken health and an energetic disposition and boundless determination to get on, had spent a morning in this way. He almost believed, as he threw himself down on the sofa and turned his eyes from the light, that he actually had been drunk (using the coarsest word, as if it had been of one of the navvies he was thinking) overnight.

And yet his heart was soft to the cause of it all. A feeling which had never been awakened in him, even when she was most kind, by his mother, which seemed out of the question so far as she was concerned, stole in with a softening influence indescribable, along with the image of that disgraced and degraded man, insensible as he seemed to his own disgrace. That easy smile of cheerful vagabondage was the only thing that threw a little light upon the unbroken gloom. It had amused John in the vagrant soul which he had taken under his wing; it was awful and intolerable to him in his father: yet unconsciously it shed a sort of faint light upon the future, from which all guidance seemed removed. What was he to do in that changed and terrible future, that new world in which there was no longer any one of all the hopes that had cheered him? Elly was gone, as far as the poles apart from him and his ways, and so were his ambitions, his schemes. There remained to him in all the world nothing but his mother and sister, who had deceived him, and whom he could now serve best by going away out of their ken for ever: and this poor criminal, abandoned by all—the convict who had no friend but Joe, who had wronged and cheated John, and brought him to the dust, but who yet was the only living creature that belonged to him and had need of him now.

He was roused from his first languor of despair (though that was a condition which could not have lasted long in any circumstances) by the entrance of the little maid to lay the table for another meal. Another meal! Was this henceforward to be the only way in which his days should be measured? But no, he said to himself, jumping up with a sort of fury from his sofa, that could not be, for there would soon be nothing to get the meals with in that case: at which thought he laughed to himself. Laughing or crying what did it matter, the one was as horrible as the other.

'Missis said as she thought perhaps you would be wishing your dinner at 'ome to-day,' said the maid, startled by his laugh.

'Oh, it doesn't matter,' said John; but, when the food came with its savoury smell, he found out, poor fellow, that he was hungry, very hungry, having eaten nothing for—he did not recollect how long, weeks it seemed to him, since that peaceful breakfast before anything had gone wrong. At twenty-one a young man's appetite cannot be quenched by anything that may happen. He ate, he felt enormously, eagerly, and afterwards he was a little better. When that was over he drew himself together, and his thoughts began to shape themselves into a more definite form.

In his profession, young as he was, he had already seen something of emigration, and had contemplated it more familiarly than is usually the case. He had been in America. He knew a little of the works that were going on in various distant regions, and he had that confidence which belongs to a skilled workman in every class, that he must find employment wherever he went. Anyhow, wherever he might decide to go, the world would be a different world for him. He would be cut off from everything with which he was acquainted or which was dear to him, as much in London as at the Antipodes. Therefore, the wiser thing was to go to the Antipodes, and make life outside at once as strange as the life within.

It would, perhaps, ease the horrible annihilation of every hope if everything external were changed, and he could imagine that it was Australia or New Zealand, and not some awful fate that had done it. And now henceforth he would have one companion—one poor companion from whom he could never cut himself free—his father! who would have to stand to him in place of a family, in place of Elly, over whom he would have to watch, whom he must never suffer to steal from his side, whom perhaps he might guide into some little tranquil haven, some corner of subdued and self-denying life where he might wear out in safety. But, alas! John recoiled with a thrill of natural horror, first at the circumstances, then at himself, for building upon that. His father was not old as fathers ought to be. He was not more than fifty, and, though this is old age to persons of twenty-one, the young man could not so far deceive himself as to see any signs of failing strength or life drawing towards its close in the man whom the austerity of prison life had preserved and purified, and whose eye danced with youthful elasticity still. He was not like an old father of seventy or eighty, the conventional father whom fiction allots to heroes and heroines, and who is likely to die satisfactorily at the end, at least, of a few years' tenderness. No. May would live, it might be, as long as his son. This was an element of despair which it was impossible to strive against, and equally impossible to confess; even to his own heart John would not confess it. It lay heavily in the depths of that heart, a profound burden, like a stone at the bottom of a well.

'Yes,' he said to himself, with a little forlorn attempt to rouse up and cheer himself on, 'to the Antipodes!' where perhaps there might be something to do, of as much importance, or more, than draining the Thames Valley: where the primitive steps of civilisation had yet to be made, and he might be of use at least to somebody. That was one thing to the good at least, to have decided so much as that. And then he seized his hat and went out. There was still one preliminary more important than any other, and that was to find the cause of all this ruin, the future object of his life. Everything else must go; his scheme—he had thrown down all his papers on the office-table, and left them there, for what was the good of them now? his love? He took up finally the letter to Elly, and with his teeth set dropped it into the box at the first post-office he came to. Having done this he stood all denuded, naked, as it were, before fate, and went forth to seek him who was the cause of it all—his father the convict; the man whom it would be his duty to serve and care for, who was all that was left to him in life.

Perhaps, if it had not been for this failure in respect to his work, for the betrayal of which he had been the victim, and the prompt discovery and consequent abandonment of him by his employers which had followed, John would not have been so certain of his duty. He never could have taken his mother's advice and altogether forsaken the father whom he had so unfortunately discovered. But he might have been induced to conceal May's existence, and to make some compromise between abandoning him altogether and burdening his life with the perpetual charge of him, as he now intended. The conjunction of circumstances, however, had narrowed the path which lay before him. Never, in any case, could he have kept Elly to the tie, which as yet was no tie, when he discovered the disgrace which overshadowed his family; and with both his great motives withdrawn—his love and his ambition—what did there remain for John? To enter with his reputation as a social traitor the service of Spender & Diggs? As soon would a soldier in the field desert to the enemy. And what, then, remained for him to do? Australia, where there was a fresh field, and where not only he but the poor burden on his life, the soiled and shamed criminal, would be unknown, and might begin again.

The first thing, however, was to find him; but John had not much doubt on that point. After a little pause of consideration he set out for Montressor's lodgings, feeling convinced that the actor would at least know where he was to be found. The Montressors, notwithstanding their return to fortune through the success of Edie, were still in the old rooms in one of the streets off the Strand, up three pairs of stairs, the same place in which John had supped upon hot sausages on his first night in London. How strange it was that an incident so trivial should have altered the colour of his whole life! For had he not, in his boyish folly, called himself John May to that chance friend, it might so have been that this discovery never would have been made. It was with a sigh that John remembered, shaking his head as he went up the long dingy stairs, that after all this had nothing to do with it, and that it was something more uncalled-for still, an accident without apparently any meaning in it, which had brought him directly in contact with his father, on the first night on which that contact was possible. The very first night! He had to break off with a sort of satirical smile at this accidental doom, when the door was opened by Mrs. Montressor, who looked at him with a startled expression, and not the welcoming look with which on his rare visits she had always met him.

'Oh, Mr. May!' she said; then paused and added, hurriedly, 'Montressor is out, and I am just going to fetch Edie from the rehearsal. I am so sorry I cannot ask you to come in.' He thought she stood against the door defending it, and keeping him at arm's length.

'It does not matter,' he said. 'I had—no time to come in. I wanted to find out from Montressor the address—of a friend.'

'What friend?' said the woman, quickly.

'He must have told you, Mrs. Montressor, of the discovery we made: that his friend May—was—my father: no more than that: though it had been kept from me and I didn't know.'

'Oh, no, Mr. Sandford,' cried Mrs. Montressor, 'that was a mistake, I am sure. You see I know your real name. I found it out long ago, but I never told Montressor. No, no, Mr. Sandford, it is all a mistake. He is no relation of yours.'

A sudden gleam of hope lit up John's mind, but faded instantly.

'He is my father,' he said, 'there can be no mistake.'

'Oh, no, no,' said the woman, beginning to cry. 'It can't be, it shan't be; there is none of that man's blood in you.'

'Hush,' said John, 'he is my father. Tell me where I can find him; that is the best you can do for me, Mrs. Montressor.'

'I can't, then,' she said, 'I don't know. I will tell you frankly he has been here, but I would not have him; I know him of old: and where he is now I don't know.'

'But Montressor knows.'

'Very likely he does. I can't tell you. He is out. I don't know where he has gone. I'll give you no information, Mr. Sandford, there! If he has the heart of a mouse in him, he will never let you know.'

'And what sort of a heart should I have if I let him elude me?' said John. 'No, if you would stand my friend, you must find him out for me. I am going abroad. I am leaving England—for good.'

'Is it for good?' said Mrs. Montressor. 'Oh, I'm afraid it's for bad, my poor boy.'

'I hope not,' said John, steadily, 'at all events it's all the good that is left me. And I cannot go without him. Tell Montressor, for God's sake, if he wants to stand my friend, to bring my father to me, or send me his address.'

It took him some time to convince her, but he succeeded, or seemed to succeed, at last. And he went away, not at all sure that the object of his search was not shut up behind the door which Mrs. Montressor guarded so carefully. He resumed his thoughts where he had dropped them, as he went down again the same dark and dingy stairs; they seemed to wait for him just at the point at which he had left off. The very first night! he almost laughed when he thought of it: and then he began to account to himself for that meeting, following up the course of events to the time of his first acquaintance with Joe. He went back upon this carelessly enough, remembering the man in the foundry at Liverpool, and before that, before that—— John started so violently that he slipped down half-a-dozen steps at the bottom of the stairs, and a sort of stupor seized his brain till he got into the open air and walked it off.

There came before him like a picture the evening walk with Mr. Cattley, the tumult outside the 'Green Man,' the half-drunken tramp who wanted some woman of the name of May. Good God! was he so near the discovery then, and yet had no notion of it! He remembered the very attitude of the man sitting with his back against the wall, maundering on in his hoarse tones, half-drunk, muddled yet obstinate, about his mate's wife and the news he was bringing. Could it be his mother—*his mother!* the fellow was seeking all the time: and had he got thus closely on the scent from some vague information about the change of habitation made by his grandparents? How strange all seemed, how impossible, and yet how natural! And to think of the boy going gravely by, disgusted yet half-amused, with his lantern, looking down from such immense heights of boyish immaculateness upon the wretched, degraded creature who played the helot's part before him, and called forth his boyish abstract protest against the cruelty of the classic moralists who thus essayed to teach their children by the degradation of others. It all came before him, every step of the road, the aspect of everything, every word almost that had passed between Mr. Cattley and himself. And all this time it was himself whom Joe was seeking, and at last—at last—his message had come home! He seemed to be gazing at the village street, and that first act of the tragedy played upon it, with a smile to himself at the strange, amazing, incredible, yet still and always so natural—oh, so natural—sequence of events—when all of a sudden his heart seemed to turn that other corner under the trees, and, with a rush of misery, it came back to him that Elly, Elly, was and could be his Elly no more.

He never knew very well how it was that he spent the rest of this long afternoon and evening. He walked about, looking vaguely for some trace of his father, or Montressor, or Joe, but saw nothing of them, as may be supposed; and then he went from shop to shop of the outfitters, where emigrants are provided with all they want on their voyage: and finally went back to his rooms, and, in the blank of his misery, went to bed, not knowing what to do.

And thus, in the changed world, in the darkened life, the evening and the morning made the first day.

CHAPTER XIV.

THE VALLEY OF HUMILIATION.

ANOTHER followed; and then another morning after that.

Night and day were much the same to John in this dreadful pause of existence. Sometimes he dozed in the day, in utter weariness and sickness of heart, after coming in from an unsuccessful search for some trace of any one of those three men who had so changed the course of his life; often lay awake through the slow and terrible night, in which all manner of miserable thoughts came crowding about him like vultures, so that he did not know which was most insupportable, the night or the day. The wondering looks of the people in the house, the shaking of the head of his landlady, Mrs. Short, who saw all her fears realised, and made no doubt whatever that John had been tempted, and had fallen, and had been dismissed by his employers with obliquy, did not affect him, for he was unconscious of them. He sought no comfort from his mother, who was the only confidant he could have had—indeed, he sought comfort nowhere. He did not recognise the possibility of any succour existing for him at all.

Again he had slept late on the morning of the third day. By that means he seemed to cheat time of one little bit of its tedious, soul-consuming power. The day was a little less long when he thus managed to steal an hour from it, and this habit, which the troubled and sorrowful share with the idle and dissipated, easily steals upon those who are unemployed and unhappy. He felt that he hated the light, as so many have done before him. To turn his face to the wall, to close his eyes upon it, to push as far from him as possible the new day, in which there could be nothing but evil, was a little gain in the dearth of all comfort. John was roused with a start by some one knocking at his door, to bid him make haste and come downstairs, where two ladies were waiting for him.

'Missis wants to know if she's to send up breakfast for them?' the serving maiden inquired.

John, in his consternation, did not answer the question. Two ladies! After a while, he said to himself, while he completed his dressing hastily, that no doubt his mother had sent for Susie, and that together they had come to plead with him to abandon the unfortunate, to keep everything secret. John smiled at himself in his glass at the thought. Abandon him! The poor culprit, the convict, the deserted father had been more magnanimous than they were, and had fled from him not to shame him. So much the less could his son abandon him. He prepared himself to tell them his resolution as he finished his dressing. Susie would cry, perhaps, but neither of them would care much: why should they care? He had never entered actively into their lives. It would be nothing to them to lose him. They might, indeed, have been proud of him, had he come to be, as he believed he should so short a time ago, a successful and famous engineer. But pride and love were two different things. They might plead as they pleased, but he would not give in to them. What, preserve this hideous secret, cheat the world into supposing them an honourable family? That might have been, perhaps, had John been entering upon a successful career, accompanied by the plaudits of the office, and with many things depending upon him. But now when nothing depended upon him, when he was considered to have justified all prejudices against him (of which now he knew the cause) and to be himself a traitor—*now* that he should shrink from doing his duty! No, no! His father after all was everything that belonged to him, as he was the only thing that belonged to his father.

He went through all this with himself as he prepared to go downstairs. And he threw himself into their thoughts. He fancied how, as they heard his step coming down, they would say over to each other the arguments it would be best to use, and the mother might perhaps suggest to Susie to be more loving than usual to win him. It was very likely that she would do that. And when John opened the parlour door and found himself in a moment caught in some one's arms, the first flush of consciousness in his mind was that to the letter the programme was being carried out.

But that flush of consciousness was very brief. The next was different, it was rapture and anguish mingled together. For the arms that were flung about him, the face that was put close to his was not his sister's but Elly's—Elly's! Good heavens!

'Don't!' he cried, putting her away from him, putting away her hands from his shoulders. 'Don't! for the love of God.'

'Jack!' she cried, 'Jack!' and kissed him determinedly, openly, without a blush, flinging off those deterring hands.

'Oh, Jack, my boy, what does all this mean?' said another voice behind. Had he gone mad, or was he still in a dream? For this mocking spirit seemed to speak with Mrs. Egerton's voice. The whole world seemed to swim in his eyes for a moment, and then things settled back into their place, and he found himself standing in his parlour with two ladies indeed, but the ladies were Elly and her aunt. Mrs. Egerton was seated in the only easy-chair in the room, the one which May the convict had preferred, and Elly stood all eagerness and life, like a creature made out of light, in the full shining of the morning sun which came in at the end window, and which had caught and translated itself bodily to her hair.

John stood apart, like the shadow of this lovely group, which was of the light, as he said to himself, and could not have too much shining upon it, while he was of the dark and could do nothing but retire into the gloom. He turned towards Mrs. Egerton with a trembling which he could not disguise.

'Why,' said he, 'did you come here? Why have you let her bring you— Why have you brought her here?'

'Jack,' said Mrs. Egerton, 'what does it all mean? Do you think anyone who cared for you as we do could be satisfied with what you said?'

'But you—didn't much care for me,' he said, feeling stupified and unable to face the real issue. She made a little gesture of impatience.

'I know you have some reason to speak. I was against you: but that's a very different thing from this. Do you think your friends could give you up when you were in trouble, my poor Jack? Oh! no! no——'

'Oh no, no, no,' echoed Elly. 'Not even papa. He said that we must come and see——'

'Yes,' cried Mrs. Egerton, 'my brother himself. He said what of course anybody would say, that to let you go off and make a martyr of yourself for some unknown reason was out of the question. He would have come himself, but you know he never goes anywhere.'

'And Mr. Cattley offered to come,' said Elly, 'but we felt that we were the right people to come, Jack.'

He stood stupified listening to the alternation of the voices, both so soft in their different tones, both—in view of him, and in the ease and everyday circumstances of his lodging, and his appearance, which was little changed—beginning to feel at their ease too, and as if nothing could be so terrible as they had supposed. It relieved their minds beyond description to see everything in the usual order of a place in which people were living. No man could be in the depths of a catastrophe who had his breakfast-table neatly set out and the *Standard* folded by his plate. 'He has given us a fright for nothing,' Elly had said. The appearance of John indeed gave them a moment's pause, for he was very pale, and his eyes had a worn and troubled look which it was impossible not to remark. But two days' illness, or the failure of his scheme, or any other trifling (as these ladies thought) matter, would have sufficed to do that. As he did not say anything, being too much confused and disturbed and miserable and (almost) happy, to do so, Mrs.

Egerton went on, in her calm voice, the voice of one who was accustomed to no infringements of the happy ordinary course of life,

'Now that we are here, don't you think you might give us some breakfast, Jack? We have travelled most part of the night.'

He went and gave the necessary orders without a word—which, however, was not necessary, for Mrs. Short herself met him in the passage, bringing up the 'things.' The sight of these visitors had at once set John right in his land-lady's mind. Mrs. Sandford, who was his ma, was a dignified functionary, and worthy of every respect, but she was still only Mrs. Sandford of the hospital: whereas the ladies who thus arrived with their travelling-bags in the early morning were ladies to their finger-tips, and had every sign of belonging to that class of the community, more respected than any other by the masses, which has nothing to do. And before he could remark upon the extraordinary position, the horror and the ridicule of it, John found himself sitting down to table with his cheerful guests, who were delighted to see that there was really nothing much to make any fuss about, and put off the explanation till after breakfast with the greatest composure, making themselves in the meantime very much at home.

Elly pried about at all his treasures, found out her own photograph in the place from which he had not removed it, shut up in a little velvet shrine—and opened his books, and took out a rose-bud from among the little knot of flowers which one of John's pensioners brought him regularly. She gave him a bright glance of love and sauciness, and put the rose into her bodice. Poor John! How happy it would have made him a week ago: what an aggravation of misery it was now: an anguish made more poignant by this mingled sweetness, which broke the poor fellow's heart.

They breakfasted, almost gaily, making even John for a moment or two forget himself. And then when the meal was over the examination began.

'Jack,' said Mrs. Egerton, 'it has been a great comfort to see you— though you wrote in such a solemn tone—looking fairly well upon the whole. Tell us, what made you do so, now?'

Elly sat down beside him, leaning against his chair.

'Yes, tell us, Jack,' she said.

She was smiling, almost laughing, at his paleness, at his trouble, with not the faintest notion what it was, or indeed that it could be anything worthy, she would have said, of 'the fright he had given them.' Her attitude, her smile, the way in which she looked at him, so tender, so saucy, so frank, overwhelmed poor John. He got up hurriedly, leaving her astonished, deserted in the place she had taken, and confronted them both in an access of self-controlled, yet impatient misery, with his back to the wall.

'I will tell you,' he said, hoarsely, 'if you insist upon it. I said so in my letter. It would have been kinder to let me go away, and take no notice. But if you insist I must explain.'

'Insist! Explain!' said Mrs. Egerton. 'How is it possible not to insist when you speak as you have done. Did you expect us really to let you break off everything and disappear without a word?'

'Mrs. Egerton,' said poor John, 'you said there was no engagement to be allowed between Miss Spencer and me.'

Elly got up at this amazed, and went and stood by him, and touched his arm with her hand. 'Oh, Jack!' she said, with a reproach which went to his heart.

'Well,' said Mrs. Egerton, 'that is true. I said I would not hear of it; but that is very different from suddenly breaking it off on the man's side, without a word.'

'Oh, very, very different!' cried Elly. 'Aunt Mary, he never, never could intend to use me so.'

It was all a sort of sweet trifling to Elly, a sort of quarrel to be made up, though without any of the harshness of a quarrel—a little misunderstanding that could only end in one way.

And he stood leaning up against the wall facing them, with his sad knowledge in his heart, knowing that it was no trifle that stood between them, but a great gulf which neither could cross. He stood and gazed at them for a moment, his eyes and his heart and every member of him thrilling with insupportable pain.

'I will tell you if you wish it,' he said. 'I don't want to tell you, but if I must, I must. I told you that I always believed my father to be dead. He was nothing but a vision to me. I remember him only as a child does. I believed he was dead.'

'Yes,' said Mrs. Egerton, interested, but mildly, while Elly continued to look up, smiling into his face.

'I remember, too,' she said, 'how he used to come in and take you out of bed.'

The unfortunate young man shuddered. It was so dreadful to think of this now, and to think that the cause of all his trouble remembered it too, as the one distinct thing when so much was blank. And to see the untroubled curiosity in their faces, so unexpectant of the thunderbolt which was about to fall!

'The reason he has been out of sight so long is—that he has been in prison for forgery for fourteen years. He came out about a month since, and I found him the first night, but without knowing who he was. He is a convict, and has been in prison for fourteen years.'

Mrs. Egerton uttered a low cry as if somebody had struck her. As for Elly, she did not understand, but looked at him again with growing wonder, as if she knew only from his face, not from what he said.

'It is easily explained, isn't it?' he said, with a strange smile; 'not much trouble, that is how it is. I knew nothing, no more than you did, or I should be inexcusable. Now you have heard it, take her away. Oh, Mrs. Egerton, now you know—spare me, and take her away.'

'Jack! God bless you, my poor boy. Oh, Jack, I never dreamt of this. God help you, my poor boy.'

'Yes, I hope He will: for nobody else can. It is like that in the prayer-book—"Because there is none other that fighteth for us." Take her away. She can't understand. Oh, Mrs. Egerton, for God's sake, take her away.'

'Yes, Jack; yes, I will; that is, I will if I can. Elly, do you hear him? He does not want us; not now, not at this dreadful moment. Oh, my poor, heart-broken boy! Oh, God help you, my poor Jack!'

Mrs. Egerton got up, as if she intended to go away; but then she stopped and held out her hands to him, and finally drew him to her, and gave him a kiss upon his pale cheek, bursting out into crying as she drew him, resisting, into her arms.

'Oh, my poor boy! oh, my poor boy! how are you to bear it?' she cried.

Oh, if he could but have put his head on her motherly bosom, and cried like a child, as even a man may do, like one whom his mother comforteth! But John, with Elly on the other side of him, resisted, and would not do this. He said, hoarsely:

'I can't bear it—I must bear it: only take her away.'

'Elly—Elly! do you hear? We make it worse for him. You and I must not make anything worse for him. Elly, let us go away.'

'It seems as if I had nothing to do with all this,' said Elly, with trembling lips. 'Yet I thought it was me you loved, and not anyone else. I thought——'

'Oh, Elly!' Mrs. Egerton cried, weeping, 'don't you see you are torturing him? Oh, I wish I knew what to do! Elly, don't you see you are breaking his heart? Come away, and leave him to himself. It is perhaps the kindest thing we can do.'

Elly did not move. She did not cry, though her lips quivered. She stood up straight by his side, as if nothing would ever alter her position.

'You may go,'she said, 'Aunt Mary. You are not so very near a relation: but I am not going, not a step. What, just when he wants me? Just when it is some good to have some one to stand by him. I shall not move, not a step. I am in my proper place. Is that all you know of Elly, Jack?'

There had been a faint tapping for some time at the door, which in the excitement and agitation of the little company within had gone on without notice. They were all too much absorbed to be conscious of it, or, if conscious, to think of it as appealing in any way to them. To John it had been a faint additional irritation, a something which penetrated through all the rest like a child crying or a door swinging, nothing that affected himself or made any call upon him. At this point, however, the patience of the applicant outside failed, the door was opened softly, and first a head put in, and then the entire person. It was Mrs. Egerton who first caught sight of this intruder. She dried her eyes hurriedly and looked, with a hasty attempt to recover her composure, at the wistful but still cheerful countenance, with a smile upon it like the smile of a child who has been punished for some fault, but comes back propitiatory, with looks intended to conciliate, and a humble yet not uncomplacent consciousness of being good, and ready to make amends. A child in such a frame of mind is always amiable, and so was, to all appearance, the man who stepped softly in, with his hat in one hand and a bundle of papers in the other. He was scarcely young enough for the pose, or for the look, or the desire to please and to be forgiven, and to make all up again, which was in every line of his face. But to Mrs. Egerton the face was a pleasant one, with a good, *innocent* expression, which made her feel that this conciliatory personage could not be a very great offender. He made her a little bow when he caught her eye, and seemed to take her into his confidence as he stood there deprecating, smiling. John did not perceive him till he had come into the room, and in the same deprecating manner closed the door behind him. Then he made a step forward, holding out the papers in his hand.

'Here,' he said, and the ladies, watching with sudden interest, were startled by the bound John made at the sound of this unexpected voice. 'Here are your papers—Mr. Sandford.' He made a little pause before the name. 'I had no right, I believe, to take them away, but at the moment it did not occur to me in that light. I thought—— ah!—no, no, that is all—nonsense. Don't think of it any more.'

For John had darted towards him, caught him by the arm, and said 'Father!' in the midst of the little speech he was making.

'No, no,' he repeated, 'that is all nonsense. Nothing of the sort, nothing of the sort. Here are your papers, which is the only thing to think of. I have brought you—your papers. That is all. I didn't intend to disturb you in the midst of your friends.'

He would have slid out again, or at least he made a semblance of wishing to slide out, though in reality his eyes were full of curiosity respecting John's friends, who on their side gazed at him with an almost ludicrous dismay. This, at least, was the feeling of Mrs. Egerton, who stood with a helpless gasp of incredulity and amazement gazing at this criminal, this untragical, unterrible apparition of whom she had been thinking a moment before with horror in which no mitigating circumstance had any part.

'I did not think,' said the culprit, with his deprecating look, 'that you would have been at home at this hour. I thought I would find the room empty when I got here. I had these back from Spender & Diggs last night. I intended only to leave them—not to disturb you among your friends.'

John's mouth was so dry that he could scarcely speak. He took May by the arm and almost forced him into a chair.

'I did not seek you,' he said, 'God knows. It would be better for us if you had been dead as I thought. But you cannot go away now on any pretext of disowning who you are. This is my father, Mrs. Egerton. I have told you who he is and what he is—there's no more to say. As for Miss—as for—for Elly—— Oh, my God!'

He stood holding his father by the arm, but with the other hand he covered his face. Such a cry of anguish could find no words except in the inevitable universal appeal which human nature takes its final refuge in, whatever its misery may be.

Even at this moment, however, the comic element, which mixes with almost every tragedy, came in when it ought least to have shown itself. May struggled against the detaining hold with a look of injured amiability and innocent amazement.

'I'm not used to be kept by force,' he said, turning to the elder lady with that look of taking her into his confidence. 'He grips me like—like a policeman. I don't know what he wants to do with me: to expose me to ladies who don't know me: to make you think—— If I've made a mistake, why, there's your papers again, and all's right between us. Let me go.'

Elly stole round to the other side of the prisoner's chair.

'Oh, sir,' she said, 'I don't know who you are: but you must stay if Jack wishes you to stay. He is unhappy, do not cross him now. If you are his father, we are your friends as well as his.'

May's countenance changed. He looked at her with an anxious, furtive pucker of his eyelids.

'Young lady,' he said, 'who are you? are you—Susie?' with a shade of sudden gravity on his face.

'No,' said Elly, casting at John a glance of radiant defiance, unable even at that moment to take his rejection seriously. 'I am—engaged to Jack.'

The man who had brought such dismay and misery with him had no lively sense of shame, but he had occasional perceptions as keen as they were evanescent. He looked for a moment at the group round him, and divined all it meant. It was not easy for the quickest wit to find a remedy.

'Madam,' he said, turning to Mrs. Egerton, 'this young man has been working too hard, and he is off his head. Take care of him. It's a common thing among inventors; take care of him.'

He settled himself on his chair as if he were about to enter on a long, peaceable explanation; then, in a moment, with the skill which is learned among criminals, he snatched his arm from John's grasp and was gone. The clang of the door as it closed behind him was almost the first notice they had that he had escaped.

John was weakened by the sufferings of the past days, and altogether taken by surprise. He was thrown against the wall, and, for a moment, stunned by the shock. Mrs. Egerton, half disposed to think the respectable visitor was right and the young man crazed—half alarmed by that sudden exit, not knowing what to do—held his hands in hers and chafed them, bidding some one fetch a doctor, send for his mother, do something—she knew not what.

CHAPTER XV.

THE FATHER AND CHILDREN.

MR. CATTLEY had quietly taken possession of Susie and her arrangements from the moment of the agitating conversation which followed John's letter to Elly. It could scarcely be said that he had intended to make a declaration of love to her—though for some time it had been apparent to him that this was the solution of all the difficulties of that disruption in his life which he had not himself done anything to bring about, yet which was natural and necessary, and a change which he could neither refuse nor draw back from when it came. The sudden rending asunder of all the bonds that had fashioned his existence for years had been very painful to the curate. To keep them up unnaturally, in defiance of separation and distance, was all but impossible, and yet to cut himself finally adrift was an operation which he knew not how to perform. Susie had given him unconsciously the key to all these difficulties. Had he remained at Edgeley, leading a somewhat pensive and unfulfilled, yet happy life, his devotion to Mrs. Egerton would have been in all likelihood enough for his subdued and moderate spirit. It was as much out of the question that she should marry him as that the sky and the fields should effect a union, or any other parallel unconjoinable things: but there was little occasion for any attempt at such an alliance, considering that the terms on which they stood, of tenderest and most delicate friendship, were enough for all requirements. It is delightful to keep up such a tie when circumstances permit, and no more strenuous sentiment breaks in—but to break it is a thing full of embarrassment and difficulty. Scarcely any woman is so unnaturally amiable as to behold the defection of her servant and knight without a certain annoyance; it is difficult altogether to forgive that self-emancipation and disenthralment; and on the other hand the very delicacy and romantic sentiment in the mind of the man which makes such relations possible fills him with trouble and awkwardness when the moment comes at which more reasonable and natural ties take the place of the Platonic bond.

Mr. Cattley had felt the crisis deeply; he had not known how to detach himself, or what to do with his life when the disruption should have been made. Susie's sudden appearance had been an inspiration and a deliverance to him. He had felt in her the solution of all his doubts. And now the sudden trouble which had come upon her, and which in his interest and long affection for John it was so natural he should share, came in like what he would himself have called 'a special providence,' to make his way more easy. That he should take her, so to speak, into his own hands, guide her, take care of her, aid her in everything that could be done for the family at such a crisis, was natural, most natural to a man of his character, most convenient in a general crisis of affairs. That he should step into the breach, that he should defend and help all who were likely to suffer, that he should manage matters for any distressed family, and specially help John, and help everybody, was what all the world expected from Mr. Cattley. It was his natural office. So that not only Susie but Susie's troubles came with the most perfect appropriateness into his life, and afforded him the opportunity of withdrawing and emancipating himself on the one hand and securing his own happiness on the other, as nothing else could have done.

This is not to say that the communication Susie had made to him about her father had been received by the curate with indifference. It had, on the contrary, given him a great shock. A convict! That he should connect himself with such a person—he, a clergyman—a man placed in a position where all his connections and relationships were exposed to scrutiny—was a thought which gave him a momentary sensation, indescribable, of giddiness and faintness and heart-sickness; but the result of this shock was an unusual one. It made him instantly commit himself— identify himself with the sufferer; take her up, so to speak, upon his shoulders and prepare to carry her through life, and save her from all effects of this irremediable misfortune. This was not the effect it would have had on ordinary men; but it was so with Mr. Cattley. The first thing to be done seemed to snatch up Susie, not to let it hurt her—not even to let her feel for a moment that it could hurt her. A convict! He remembered the story faintly when he heard the name, how it had a certain interest in it, in consequence of the character of the man, whom everybody liked, although the forger had ruined his family, and plunged all belonging to him into misery. And to think now, after so many years, that he himself was to be one of the people plunged into trouble by this criminal of a past time! The shock went through his nerves and up to his head like a sudden jar to his whole being. But there was perhaps something in his professional habit of finding a remedy for the troubles brought under his eye, the quick impulse of doing something, which becomes a second nature with the physicians of the spirit as well as with those of the body, which helped him now. And then it afforded him the most extraordinary and easy opening out of a difficult conjunction of affairs; that had to be taken into account—as well as the rest.

The result was that Mr. Cattley took Susie to London to her mother, and at once, without anything—or at least very little more—said, took his place as a member of the family, threatened with great shame and exposure through the return of the disgraced father, whom some of them had hoped never to see again, and some had no knowledge of. Nobody but a clergyman could have done this so easily, and even Mrs. Sandford, with all her pride and determination to share the secret with no one, could not refuse the aid of a cool head and sympathetic mind in the emergency in which she found herself placed. She was too much pre-occupied by her great distress to have much leisure of mind to consider this sudden new arrival critically as Susie's suitor. At an easier moment that question would no doubt have been discussed in all its bearings—whether he was not too old for Susie; whether he was not very plain, very quiet; whether they had known each other long enough; whether they suited each other: all these matters would have afforded opportunity of discussion and question. But in the present dreadful emergency there was no time for any such argument.

'Susie has accepted me for her husband,' Mr. Cattley said (which, indeed, Susie had scarcely done save tacitly), 'what can I do to help you?' There seemed nothing strange in it. It was his profession to have secrets confided to him, to help all sorts of people. Even Mrs. Sandford could not resist his quiet certainty that their affairs were his, and that he could be of use. And he had all the strength and freshness of a new agent, impartial, having full command of his judgment. He had none of John's stern and angry Quixotism and determination not to lose hold again of the father who was a disgrace to him, that fiercest development of duty—neither did he share the horror and loathing of the wife for the man who had betrayed and disgraced her. He was of Mrs. Sandford's mind that the culprit should be kept apart, that no attempt should be made to reinstate him in the family; and he was of John's mind that May could not be abandoned. He agreed and disagreed with both, and he was sorry for all—at once for the family driven to horror and dismay by such a sudden apparition, and for the unfortunate criminal himself, thus cut off from all the ties of nature.

Susie took no independent action in the matter. She left it now to him, as she had left it all her life to her mother, feeling such questions beyond her, she who was so ready and so full of active service in the practical ways of life. She left the decision to those who were better able to make it, but with an altogether new and delightful confidence such as she had never known before; for Mr. Cattley was far more merciful than anyone who in Susie's experience had ever touched this painful matter. Mrs. Sandford had desired nothing so much as never to hear the name of the husband through whom she had suffered so many humiliations and miseries again; but Mr. Cattley would not permit the natural right to be shaken off, or the claims of blood abandoned. Susie turned to him with a gratitude which was beyond words in her mild eyes. Her mother's panic and loathing were cruel, but he was ever kind and just. She looked at him with that sense that he was the best of created beings, which it is so expedient for a wife to possess. Even love does not always carry this confidence with it, but Susie was one of the women who will always, to the last verge of possibility, give that adoration and submission to the man upon whom their affections rest. And happily she had found one by whom, as far as that is possible to humanity, they were fully deserved.

They set out together in the morning sunshine, after many arguments and consultations with Mrs. Sandford, to seek John in his lodgings and settle if possible upon some common course of action. But, though so many painful questions were involved, these two people were able to dismiss them as they walked along together. They seemed to step into a land of gentle happiness the moment they were alone with each other, though in the midst of the crowded streets. They went across the bridge making momentary involuntary pauses to look at the traffic on the river, forgetting that they ought not to have had any attention to spare for such outside matters. Though Susie was entirely town-bred, they looked what they were henceforward to be—a country pair, a rural couple come up from their vicarage to see the world. There ought not to have been so much ease, so much sweetness in the morning to May the convict's daughter: and yet she could not help it, there it was. And to Mr. Cattley, who had always been accustomed to a somewhat secondary place, the sensation of being supreme was strangely delightful. A woman who can give that unquestioning admiration, that boundless trust, is always sweet. It is not every woman that can do it, however godlike may be the man: and the curate did not believe that he was godlike. But yet it was very delightful that she should think so. It was a surprise to him to receive this tender homage; but it was very sweet.

They had reached the quiet street in which John's rooms were, when Susie was suddenly roused out of this heavenly state by the sight of some one coming hastily out of her brother's door. They were still at a sufficient distance to see that he came out half-running, as if pursued, and that he looked round him with alarm as he came towards them, stumbling a little with uncertain steps. Something perhaps it was in this somewhat wavering movement which roused old recollections in her mind—and her father, but for that temporary lapse into personal blessedness, had been very much in the foreground of her imagination.

She let go Mr. Cattley's arm with a shock of sudden awakening, with a cry of 'Papa!' She recognised him in a moment. He was in reality very little changed, far less changed than she was, the austerity of his prison life having preserved the freshness of early years in his face.

'Papa,' she said, and stopped and reddened with sudden emotion, ashamed to look at him who she thought must stand abashed before her, and for the first time fully apprehending this tragedy, which no one could smooth away.

'Eh!' he cried, and gave her a hurried look. 'I am in a great hurry. I can't speak to you now:' then he stopped reluctantly, for the first time realising what she had said. No, it was not shame; he was not afraid of meeting her eye: but a look of curiosity and interest came into his face. 'What's that you are calling me? Do you know me? Who are you? Are you——? is this Susie?' he said.

'Oh, yes, papa, it is Susie. Don't go away. We were coming to look for you, to ask—don't go away from us. You are not at all changed,' she said, putting out her hands to detain him, 'you are just the same. Papa, oh, where are you going? Don't go away.'

'You think so? Not changed! I might be—for you are changed, Susie, and so is the world; everything's changed. Don't stop me, I must go; your brother, if that is your brother—and if you are Susie——'

'Have you seen John, papa?'

'John,' he repeated, with a half smile; and, though he had been in such haste, he stopped now at once with every appearance of leisure. 'He may be John, but he's not Johnnie, my little boy. He's like a policeman,' he went on, in a tone of whimsical complaint, rubbing his arm where John had grasped him; 'he clutches in the same way. My little chap would never have behaved like that. And so you're Susie? I see some likeness now. You were your mother's pet, and the boy was mine. Ah! well, it comes to the same thing in the end. You're both of you ashamed of me now.'

'Oh, papa,' cried Susie, with tears, 'don't say so; don't think so! John——'

'Yes, I know: he wants to get hold of me, to keep me in some family dungeon where I can't shame him. I know that's what he wants. No, child, I'm going away. Do I want to disgrace you? I'll go, and you shall never hear of me more.'

'Papa,' cried soft-voiced Susie, 'come back and let us talk all together like one family. Come back to poor John's lodgings. We are all one family, after all. We are all friends. Oh, come back, come back, papa!'

'He has got ladies there—the girl he is going to marry. Never, never! I'm not going to have anything to do with him. I'm glad to have seen you, Susie. God bless you, you've got a sweet face. You're like a sister of mine that died young. If you ever see your mother—I suppose you see your mother sometimes?—you can tell her—— Well, perhaps I gave her reason to hate me and give up my name. You can tell her she'll never be troubled anymore with me.'

'Oh, papa!' Susie drew a long breath and held him firmly by the arm. 'Here is John. You must speak to John.'

John had come hurriedly up to the other side, having followed from his house, and now put his hand also upon his father's arm.

'I can't let you out of my sight,' he said, breathlessly. 'We must understand everything, we must settle everything now.'

'Oh, listen to him, papa: it's not his fault; let us consult together; we are all one family. Surely, surely we are all friends,' Susie cried.

May stood between his children with a sullenness unusual to it coming over his face. He shook off John's hold pettishly.

'I told you he clutched like a policeman,' he said. 'I don't mind you, Susie, you're natural. If I had you with me, I might perhaps—— But it's no use thinking of that. You can tell your mother that whatever happens she shall never be troubled with me.'

'Father,' said John, with a shudder at the word, 'we none of us want to neglect our duties. Now that you are here, you can't disappear again. We belong to each other whether we wish it or not. You have a claim upon us, and we—we have a claim upon you. Come back. Susie, get him to come back.'

A look of panic came upon May's face. He shook them off from either hand.

'Don't let us have a row in the street,' he cried. 'You'll bring all the policemen about. And when a man has once been in trouble they always think it's his fault. Let me go.'

'Not without telling us where to find you, at least,' said John.

'Oh, papa, papa!' said Susie. 'Don't go, don't go.'

'We'll have all the policemen in the place about,' May said, looking round him with alarm.

Mr. Cattley had stood by all the time saying nothing. He came forward now, and drew John aside.

'Jack, will you leave it in my hands?' he said. 'I know everything, more perhaps than you do. And you're not in a condition to judge calmly. You know you can trust me.'

'And who may this be now?' said May, in a pettish and offended tone. He turned to the new speaker with a rapid change of front: but changed again as soon as he perceived what the new speaker was. He had known a great many chaplains in his time, and had never found them unmanageable. 'I see you're a clergyman,' he said, in his usual mild tones: 'and you have a good countenance,' he added, approvingly. 'There's some little questions to settle between me and—my family. I don't mind talking of our affairs with such a—with such a—respectable person. So long as no attempt is made on my personal freedom.' He paused a little, and then laughed with his usual perception of the ludicrous. 'I'm very choice over that,' he said, 'it's been too much tampered with already.' He looked from one to another as he spoke, with a faint expectation of some smile or response to his pleasantry: some sense of the humour of it in Susie's deprecating anxious face or the stern misery of John. The want of that reply chilled him for a moment, but only for a moment. Then he stepped out briskly from between his irresponsive children.

'Lead on—as Montressor would say—I'll follow with my bosom bare—or at least with my heart open—which comes to the same thing, I suppose,' he said.

This transaction took place so rapidly that John, in his confused state, and even Susie, scarcely understood what was taking place till they found themselves alone, watching the two other figures going quickly and quietly along the street. To Susie it seemed as if in a moment everything had come right. Mr. Cattley carried off her anxieties with him, to be solved in what was sure to be the best way. She came close to John's side and put her arm within his, supporting him with her confidence and certainty that all would now go well, supporting him even physically with the soft backing-up which he wanted so much. They stood together silent, watching the other two disappear along the street. How it was that John gave in so easily, and let the matter be taken out of his hands, no one ever knew; the secret was that he was worn out with misery and unrest. Body and soul had become incapable of further exertion, even of further suffering. The only solution possible to his strained nerves and strength was this—that some one else should do it for him. For he was incapable of anything more.

CHAPTER XVI.

THE GREAT SCHEME.

AND yet there was something for which the poor young fellow was capable still.

While this strange meeting had gone on, a telegraph boy—that familiar, common-place little sprite of the streets—had made his way to John's door; and, unnoticed by the agitated group, had been directed by Mrs. Short putting out her head and shaking it sadly all the time by way of protest—to where John stood. This little bit of side action had been going on for a minute or two without anyone observing it; and it was not till the group had broken up and John and his sister were standing together, incapable of speech and almost of thought, watching the others as they walked away, that the telegraph boy came up and thrust his message into John's hand. It seemed a vulgar interruption, breaking into the tragic scene; and John stood with the envelope in his hand, with a sense that he was as much beyond the reach of any communications which could reach him in that way, as if he had come to himself in the land beyond the grave. But Susie felt differently; the interruption was to her a welcome break.

'Look at it,' she said, holding his arm close with a woman's keen interest in a new event. 'It may be something of importance.'

'There is nothing of any importance,' he said, in the deadly languor of exhaustion. 'Nothing can make any difference to us now.'

'But open it,' said Susie.

He gave her a look of reproach. What did it matter? If the telegram had been from the Queen, it could have made no difference. Nothing could alter the fact that he was his father's son.

'But open it,' Susie said again.

He tore it open in a languid way, hoping nothing, caring for nothing, in the blank of despondency and helplessness. Even the words within did not rouse him. He read and crumpled it up in his hand.

'What is it, John?'

'Nothing very much. They want me—in the office,' he said.

'In the office! That makes me think—John, why are you here at this time of day?'

'If you mean why am I not there—— I haven't been there for three days. I have left the office,' said John, in the carelessness of his exhausted state.

She caught his arm again with an almost shriek of dismay.

'Left the office! when it is all you have to look to. Oh, John, John!'

'What did it matter? They were very unjust: they made a false accusation: and then I discovered *him*. I found out why they suspected me, why I have been suspected all my life—even by you and—my mother, Susie.'

'Oh, no, John. Oh, no, no, dear John. Never, never!' cried Susie, vehemently. 'Mother has suffered a great deal: she can't forget: she can't forgive even as we do. We do, John, don't we? We do, we do!'

'Forgive whom? The people that had always doubted me for a reason I didn't even know?'

His face grew stern. He could say nothing of the other, whom it was both easier and harder to forgive. Susie did not dare to enter upon that subject. She gave his arm a little pressure, and said, softly,

'Since they send for you, you will go, John? Oh, go! You must not throw everything away, because——'

'Because—it does not matter to anybody, least of all to me. I'll go away to America, or somewhere, and take that poor wretch, that light-hearted wretch——'

'Oh, John, he is your father.'

'I know: can you say anything worse? are you trying what is the hardest thing you can say?'

'Oh, John!' said poor Susie, and began to cry.

Her confusion, and trouble, and anxiety, not unmixed with a little exasperation, too, were not to be expressed in any other way.

He relented a little at the sight of her tears.

'I think there's no heart left in me,' he said. 'I make everybody that cares for me unhappy. You, out here in the street, and there, inside—Elly.'

'Elly!'

Susie's astonishment was so great that she could not find another word to say.

'*She* does not cry,' said poor John. 'She has come to stand by us. She is braver than I am. She's so innocent, Susie, she doesn't know. If she knew better, if she knew the world, she wouldn't come to me, a poor, shamed, and ruined man, a convict's son.'

'Oh, John!' There being no answer to make to this, Susie recurred to the former subject. He had still the telegram crushed in his hand. 'That is not about ruin and shame,' she said. 'John, tell me, what does it say?'

'I scarcely know what it says,' he answered, with an impatient sigh. And then suddenly, in a moment, by some strange miracle of the nerves and brain, he seemed to see the message glow out in big letters of flame quivering through the air, obliterating the shabby walls and long lines of the pavement, throwing a strange light upon everything—till they got inside his very soul, and obliterated everything else that was there. Words which were not divine, nor even very elevated that they should have moved him so. '*Scheme very promising, your presence indispensable.*' What did that mean? He knew very well what it meant—that all was not over, as he thought, that life and hope still remained. What did he care about such empty, impotent things? But so it was. All was not over, though he insisted within himself that it was so. The story of May and his little boy might, after all, be but a fairy-tale that had no sequence or meaning. And he was John Sandford, and the ball was at his foot once more.

John scarcely knew how he got to the office on that eventful morning; but somehow, by force or sweet persuasion, or something that drew him in spite of himself, he went, leaving the ladies still in his parlour, where, in the sickness of his heart, he could not see them again. The sight of Elly was more than he could bear. It was easier to face the Barretts, and anything they could say to him, than to look at Elly in her ignorance and certainty, in her all-confident love and courage. She to stand by him! who would not be permitted to soil her gentle name and stainless record by the most distant contact with his shame and wretchedness. Elly! her very name gave him a sick pang of mingled sweetness and misery. To think she should be ready to do all that for him—and to think that in honour and justice he ought never to see her again!

He found the Barretts, father and son, awaiting him with apparent anxiety. They both looked up eagerly when he opened the door, and Mr. William came forward, holding out his hand.

'Sit down, Sandford. My father and I wish to have a little talk with you. We are all sorry for the misunderstanding that occurred when you were here last.'

'I don't think there was any misunderstanding. Mr. Barrett told me that I was doing what he always expected, when I behaved like a traitor and liar.'

'It was all a mistake, Sandford. I give you my word it was all a mistake. Father, you had better speak for yourself.'

'I withdraw what I said, if I said that,' said the old gentleman. 'Perhaps I have been prejudiced. My opinion is that children are what their parents make them: but circumstances alter cases. And I hear from William——'

'The fact is,' said the junior partner, laying his hand upon the papers on the table, 'that this is a most remarkable scheme of yours, Sandford.'

In whatsoever depths a man may be, to have his work or his invention praised will make his heart jump. Suddenly it seemed to John as if a great cloud, which had enveloped the world, opened and rolled aside, and out from behind it, in all the splendour of day, appeared for a moment the smiling blue. He thought that cloud and darkness had been the shadow of his father; but that it was not this alone was evident suddenly now—if only for a moment. He did not say anything in reply, but drew a long breath.

'Spender & Diggs,' continued Mr. William Barrett, 'like idiots as they are, tell Prince that they can't make head or tale of it: that it's mixed up with clever things and nonsense; and that they have sent it back.'

'The man,' said John, with a stammering in his voice which his late masters thought was due to some sense of delinquency; 'the man who copied my papers, and who took them without my knowledge, went for them yesterday and demanded them back.'

'Ah, that explains——! Well, Sandford, most likely we were wrong altogether. I find a great deal that is admirable in your scheme. We see business in it,' said Mr. William, rubbing his hands. 'We see money in it. We see our way to making a great thing of it; that's the fact, Sandford. We never meant you to take our remonstrance as bitterly as you did, you know: never. Things looked bad. It looked like an ugly piece of business—it looked like——'

'Put it in plain words,' said John, roused to all his old indignation, and using involuntarily the words his navvies might have used. 'You thought it as mean a dirty trick as ever was played?'

Mr. William Barrett paused a little and then he burst into a laugh which carried off a good deal of annoyance and something like shame.

'We needn't quarrel about words,' he said, 'but I never believed it in my heart. I looked for some explanation from you that would clear it up at once, for I knew you were not the man to do a dirty trick. But I could get nothing out of you, not even when I went to your rooms that time, and found you involved deeper and deeper.'

'When did you come to my rooms?' said John, looking at him blankly.

'Sandford,' said the younger Barrett, 'look here, my good fellow, you're young and you must be careful. Whatever you have been doing, it must have been worse than an ordinary spree.'

John stared at him for a moment without comprehending: and then he answered; with a kind of smile,

'Yes, it was much worse than an ordinary—spree.'

'If it were not that I never knew you to do anything of the kind before—— Yes, I was there; you had two men with you, and I didn't like the looks of them. Now, look here: I didn't understand then, and I don't inquire now, what was the matter; you've always been a steady fellow so far as we have known; you'll have to be so more than ever, mind you, if you go into this big thing. The thing's so big that it will make your fortune—with the help our experience can give you—and if it's accepted, as I have little doubt it will be. But you'll have to be careful. Bad company and bad hours, and that sort of thing, will never do for a rising man.'

John made no reply. Bad company! yes, it had been bad company. It was hard to sit quietly under an imputation which went so entirely against all the traditions of his life, but it was better perhaps that they should think so than that they or anyone should know the truth.

The elder Mr. Barrett shook his solemn head like a wise old sheep, with his white hair and beard.

'Depend upon it,' he said, 'without good principles, no man ever did anything. Clever notions are all very well, but without good principles——'

'It's well to have the notions and the principle too,' said the junior partner, interrupting hastily. 'Here are some jottings I have put on paper, Sandford. You can run your eye over them. That's what, in case your plan should be accepted, we would propose. You had better think it well over and consult your friends: and in the meantime make use of any assistance you want in the office to put it all in right form. If you will take my advice, you will lose no time.'

John looked over the paper put into his hand with a dimness in his eye and a throbbing in his head, as if all the machinery that would be wanted in the work had suddenly been set going in his brain. It clanged, and whirred, and rang as if all the great wheels were going and the pistons falling, and every motive power in action; and then there suddenly rolled out before him like a panorama the future life which he had planned and hoped, the great works in which his mind should be the directing force, and all the industries that depended thereupon. It was not, perhaps, what the youthful dreamer would ordinarily think a romantic picture. He seemed to see all the great workshops, the men in the foundries in the glare of their red furnaces, the brickworks, the regiments of excavators on the soil, a whole busy world of men, with plenty and prosperity around them. He saw all this in one lightning flash. This was what had set his imagination soberly aflame when he was a boy. This was the lighthouse that Elly had shaped among the boundless possibilities of life in Mr. Cattley's study. Elly! Ah! that drove away his dream in a moment, and brought him back to himself, standing in a great confusion of being in Mr. Barrett's office, studying the paper—the paper which was only half visible to him, which made fortune and favour sure.

'I'll take to-day,' he said. 'I don't think I can settle to anything to-day.'

They shook hands with him, even the old sheep, looking out with his white locks with an immovable face still distrustful of John, yet compelled to that complaisance; and he went out with *that* in his pocket—that which proved his early dreams to be real, which was the test and touchstone of his value in the eyes of those who had been his masters, and were best able to judge. He went out, forgetting everything else that had happened, taking up for the moment his life where he had dropped it a week before. A week ago he would have taken that paper to the family at the rectory, and the humbleness of his origin—his origin, which was so respectable, yet not on the level of the Spencers—would have been forgotten. Again for one moment more the elation of his success got into John's brain. Again he trod on air. He thought, his brain all dizzy with the sudden rapture, of showing it all to Elly, making her understand. She would not understand, but she would think she did, in her heart, if not in her brain, and would jump to the delight of it, and all that would follow. They would say to each other that this was the lighthouse, the first idea that had struck their youthful fancy, Elly's lighthouse, which had caught John's imagination in its earliest dawning, and flashed at last into this great thing.

The young man in his misery had a revelation, a vision of overpowering sweetness and delight. Without that spark of divine light from her, he said to himself, it would never have been, this great work, which he knew would bring comfort and well-being over a whole district, and make his name famous, and bring many a blessing: *his* name; but they should know, everybody should know that by himself he never would have thought of it, that it was Elly who had been the first. How could he let the world know that it was Elly who was the first—not, indeed, to think of the Thames Valley and its drainage, or how to make an end of the floods, she who could not, God bless her, manage her algebra even, or work out a problem to save her life—but only to light up the thoughts that were good for that sort of thing, to light the first divine beacon of which all lighthouses were only the development? He was very young in spite of all his maturity and experience; and for one blissful moment, nay hour, this elation and rapture took possession of his soul, and made him forget the horrible passage through which he had gone, and all the bitter realities around him. He floated once more into a world of light and brightness, and boundless hope and enthusiasm. All the more heavenly, for the depth of despair in which he had been dwelling, was the glory of this, the confidence, the anticipation of everything that was best both in work and in life, the happiness of carrying it all out, the delight of talking it over with Elly, explaining it all to her day by day. She would not understand, not a bit, he said to himself, with tears of pleasure in his eyes; but it would come to the same thing: for she would understand him and what he wanted, and it would be her work as well as his—Elly's lighthouse, of which the foundations were laid in Mr. Cattley's study long ago.

When suddenly, in the midst of all these delightful thoughts, John felt himself struck down as if by a great stone, as if it were some falling meteor, compounded of infernal elements, though coming from the skies. It came down, down with the straight and cruel velocity which is given by natural laws, down to the very bottom of his heart. Suddenly there seemed to appear before him old Barrett shaking his head, and his own mother, with her suspicious, troubled eyes, watching him, looking for evil: and the reason of it all. The convict's son! with the whole world watching to see when the leaven would break out in him, his father's nature, the instincts of the criminal—and even his friends standing apart in horror and pity, broken-hearted, yet holding his shame aloof. What could they do but hold him aloof? And Elly, Elly, who wanted to stand by him, who had come to give him her support, to be his champion, his stainless white protector! He heard himself laugh in the street like a madman, laugh aloud with misery, he who had been nearly weeping with pleasure. God help him, for what could man do for him; or woman either, or fool, or angel—for was not she all these together, she who could dream of the possibility of standing up for him still, standing by him, and he his father's son?

- 115 -

CHAPTER XVII.

ELLY'S PLEDGE.

MRS. EGERTON and Elly were aware, but vaguely, that something was happening outside while they sat half frightened, bewildered, not knowing what to think, in John's little parlour, dismayed by the sudden appearance and disappearance of the man who was his father, who had looked at them with that deprecating, good-humoured face, unlike a criminal, and who yet was—something that they shuddered to think of. They sat there silent, listening, waiting for John to come back; but they forgave him that he did not come back. Everything was so disorganised, so out of gear, that all the ordinary laws seemed suspended, and even Mrs. Egerton forgave, indeed scarcely thought of, this breach of all the rules of courtesy. Poor boy! whatever he had done, she would have forgiven him. She was sorry for him, sorry to the bottom of her heart. And fortunately they neither of them knew that Susie had been there, and had fled, afraid to meet them, not knowing what to say to them. Both pride and honour had kept them from looking out, from spying upon John, or watching what he was doing. They had sat, as it were, behind a veil, and only known vaguely and half by instinct that another scene in this painful little drama was going on outside. And then silence had come, the sound of the voices had died away, and they had still sat looking at each other with everything stopped and arrested round them, not knowing what to think. It was some time before they made up their minds to go, leaving the address of the house in which they were in the habit of staying when they came to town to see the pictures or do a little shopping such as ladies from the country love. But all these pleasant usages were forgotten in the excitement of this crisis.

'Tell Mr. Sandford we shall expect him as soon as he can come to us.'

'Oh, I will, ma'am, I will,' cried Mrs. Short, 'for he have need of his friends, that I'm sure of. He do have need of his true friends.'

Mrs. Egerton was too much subdued and anxious even to take advantage of this opportunity to inquire into John's habits and mode of life, which for a lady accustomed to manage a parish was wonderful, and showed how serious the emergency was. And then they got into their cab and drove away.

These two ladies had come to London in a flush of tender impulse and kindness, even Mrs. Egerton, who was an impulsive woman, forgetting all her objections—which, indeed, from the beginning her heart had fought against. And the thought of John in what seemed an abyss of despair which had roused Elly to a swift determination to suffer no more interference, to go to him, stand by him, marry him even in spite of himself, and whether he wished it or not, had also swept all prudential sentiments out of the warm heart of her aunt. They had rushed like a couple of doves flying to save some wounded eagle, like a couple of generous, inconsequent women, determined that there was nothing in heaven or earth that could not be overcome by their support and love. He had been met by some sudden obstacle, perhaps, to the success he had dreamt of—good heavens, what did that matter? And as for his father, *his father*, what could he have to do with it? Even now, when they knew all, though the elder woman had met the revelation with a shriek of dismay, Elly remained stolidly, stupidly unconscious of any force in it. It did not affect her intelligence at all: if it was anything, it was a reason for standing more determinedly, more constantly, by Jack, who wanted support—that was all. It was not even that she would not permit herself to see the force of it: she did not, actually. It passed by her intelligence, and did not touch her. The more reason to stand by Jack! that was all that Elly saw.

But as they drove along in the dingy cab, through the endless shabby streets, in the silence which was rendered more complete by the din and tumult of London round them, a better understanding came to both—even Elly began to find a tremor seize her. Her mind began to work in spite of herself. The moment that crime comes near, within the circle where honour has been always a foregone conclusion, and any infringement of the law a thing impossible, is a moment unspeakable, indescribable. It is bad enough when vice shows itself among all the pure traditions of an honourable family: but crime—something that cannot be excused by the force of temptation, that cannot be wept over as affecting the sinner only, who is nobody's enemy but his own—but a breach of honesty, a crime against the law and against the rights of others! There are sins which are a thousand times more deeply guilty than theft or even forgery, but they are in a different category. Trial, conviction, the contamination of a prison, the felon's obliteration from personality and right, make up a horror and shame of the actual, undeniable, matter-of-fact kind, which the dullest feel, and which affect the innocent with a sensation like a nightmare.

In the silence of their long drive Mrs. Egerton repeated now and then to herself, 'A convict!' with a shudder. Anything but that; if the father thus suddenly discovered had been a beggar, if he had been a poor broken-down drunkard, a reprobate! There are drunkards and reprobates, alas! everywhere, whom the best of families have to put aside into some corner, and veil with silence or with pitiful excuses, with abandonment or sacrificing love. But a convict cannot be hid. A man may live the purest life, he may win everything that energy and even genius can secure, but at the end of all the meanest may rise up and say, 'Behold the convict's son,' and cover even a hero with shame. Imagination could not go so far as that in picturing the evils that are possible. Poor Jack! Poor boy! with his father a convict—a convict! The horror of it was so great and terrible that nothing was possible, save to say over and over these words of shame.

And Elly felt it still more deeply in her way. It seemed to ache all over her, this consciousness which she could never shake off, never forget. She took it for her own without doubt or question, embraced it, drew it close to her, with all the *abandon* of youth. It seemed to Elly that nobody would ever forget it, that it would be blazoned on Jack, and all who belonged to them, on their name, their dwelling, and, above all, on those great things that he was to do. And, of course, he could not give up his father; he must live with them, be their daily companion, this man who had spent years and years in a prison. She was silent, too, with a chill upon all her thoughts. No idea of deserting him ever came into Elly's mind. She accepted the misery as for her too. And all the accounts she had ever heard of the cruelty of the world in visiting disgrace upon the innocent came into her mind. Could they live it down? she asked herself, or must Jack, poor Jack, dear Jack, with only her to console him, live under this shadow, this awful, undeserved shadow, all his life?

Things were better when they got to their rooms, where all was quiet, as quiet as a London street can ever be; and where, as they sat down facing each other with nothing to do, the irrepressible controversy broke forth:

'Your father will never, never hear of it,' Mrs. Egerton said. 'Never! Even I myself, Elly—— A convict—how could we let you connect yourself with a convict? And your father and brother both clergymen! Percy would die first. I am sure he would see you die first. And even your father: your father—can be very decided when he takes a thing into his head.'

'You said so before, Aunt Mary. You said you never would consent; but you talk now as if you would have consented; as if you had consented.'

'Ah, that was very different!' Mrs. Egerton said. And in her heart Elly felt that it was different, oh, how different! So different, that even Elly herself felt with a shudder that something was before her quite other than love and happiness. There would still be love, oh, more than ever! but bitter with pain and shame.

It was the afternoon when John came to them. They perceived at once, with their quick, feminine habit of reading the face and its expression, that some change had occurred since the morning. Elly rushed to meet him, when he entered, with both her eager hands held out, but John turned from her, shaking his head with sorrowful self-control. He came and sat down opposite Mrs. Egerton. And there followed a moment in which no one spoke. Mrs. Egerton lifted up her hands, and clasped them together with the natural eloquence of restrained emotion.

'Oh, Jack,' she said, shaking her head, 'oh, my poor boy!'

Pity, tenderness, reluctance, the inexorable impossible were in her looks. It could not be, it could not be; and yet it broke her heart to say so; in such moments there is little need of words.

'I want to tell you,' he said. 'I want to show you——' He took Mr. Barrett's paper from his pocket, and spread it out before them: the figures on it were like hieroglyphics in the women's eyes. 'This is what I hoped for,' he said, 'when I left Edgeley that day—— I don't know how long ago, it might be a century. My great scheme, that I had all my heart in, is to be carried out. It will bring me a fortune: it is a great work, a work any man might be proud to do. I have got my foot on the ladder, sure. It is not mere hope any longer, but sure, as sure as anything that is mortal can be.'

'Oh, Jack!' cried Elly, rushing to his side once more.

'I am very glad, Jack,' said Mrs. Egerton, with a trembling voice, 'very glad, very glad, for you—but, oh, my poor boy——'

'I know,' he said. 'Are you glad, indeed? that's very good of you. I'm not glad, not a bit. It doesn't matter. I'll work at it all the same, but I don't care. It's the same thing to me whether it goes on or whether it stops. You need not shake your head, for I know—I know it makes no difference. But I thought I must come and tell you. I am going to make my fortune: but it does not matter to anyone in the wide world, and I don't care.'

'Jack,' said Elly, standing by his side, 'have you made up your mind that you will pay no attention to what I think or what I say?'

He looked at her in such a bewildering passion of misery and hopelessness that all expression seemed to have gone out of his eyes.

'Yes,' he said, 'I can't, I can't—even if you would.' Then he paused, drawing a breath which was half choked by something hysterical in his throat. 'But I had to come and tell you. It's what we used to talk of long ago. It's—it's the lighthouse, Elly!' he cried, with a sudden sob which all the manhood of twenty-one could not restrain, and buried his face in his hands.

She flung her arms round him, bent down over him, holding his bowed head to her breast. She was half-sister, half-mother, protector, guardian, as well as his love. Tender, domestic affection, unabashed, as well as the strong passion of the woman, shone in the eyes with which she turned to the weeping spectator.

'Do you think you or anyone will ever part me from Jack?' she said.

'Oh, children, do not break my heart! Your father will never, never consent—and Percy—and everybody who knows. Jack, for pity's sake, tell her, tell her! She will listen, perhaps, to you.'

It was a minute at least, a long, long time, before John raised himself, detaching those dear arms.

'Elly,' he said, 'I am my father's son. People have distrusted me all my life, and I never knew why. They may distrust me yet, and I will know the reason, and God knows what it may make of me. No, I know that your father will not consent.'

'And a girl's own mind is nothing,' she cried, indignant, 'I know you all think so, whatever you may say.'

John turned to Mrs. Egerton with a piteous look.

'It is you that must tell her,' he said, 'how can I do it? I'm young, too. I only know you mustn't decide, Elly, at your age. You don't know the world; you don't know what you're doing. If everything had been straightforward with me, you are still above me, gentlefolks, while I am nobody. You said so——'

'Oh, Jack, Jack!' said Mrs. Egerton, as if this was a reproach.

'Everything is straightforward with you,' said Elly. She had drawn away from him with a little movement of pride. 'But,' she said, 'it is true enough. I don't know the world, and neither do you. Perhaps we are too young. If you say that, or if Aunt Mary says that, I will not make any objection, Jack—how should I? I don't want to force you to—to have me before the time——'

The extreme youth of both gave them a simplicity of words and good faith which elder lovers could not have ventured on. He accepted what she said in all seriousness and humility.

'But there's more than that,' he said. 'Oh, Elly, I can't deny it, I can't disguise it, there's more than that. If it was only that we were too young! But everything is against us. And how could I, loving you all my life, owing everything to you as I do——'

'You owe me nothing, nothing, Jack! It is all the other way.'

'Ah, don't say that, for I know better. I was just thinking—it's all you, Elly. I should have gone into an office, or wherever they pleased to put me.

I should not have minded. It was all your lighthouse. And to think,' said Jack, as if that furnished him with a new argument, 'that I should bring you to shame! Never, Elly; I would rather die.' He paused a moment and shook his head. 'It's no good talking of dying, is it, at my age? I'd rather—live alone as I've always done, and do my work the best I could, and agree that there was nothing more for me in this world.'

'Jack!' cried Elly, with a kind of shriek of exasperation and tenderness and contradiction; and then she turned from him, her eyes flaming bright under the dew of tears, her cheeks like two deep roses, her mouth quivering, smiling, touched with fine scorn. She wanted some one to vent her loving wrath, her disdain of all mean arguments, her boundless, fiery indignation upon. 'Aunt Mary,' she cried, 'how dare you to say so, or to think it? My father is a gentleman! He may not be much as a parson—it's not for me to say: but he's as fine a gentleman as Chaucer's knight. Say all the bad things you please, you two, I know what's in papa! He will no more forbid me to marry John than he would turn against the poor boy himself for what's no fault of his. But I won't do it now,' Elly added, magnanimously, breaking into a laugh, which much resembled crying. 'Not now. I'll wait till I'm one-and-twenty. And then I'll do it with my father's full consent, whatever you may do or say, you two!'

With which defiance flung at them, Elly majestically marched out of the room, leaving them to conclude the conference together. What she did after, whether she did anything but retire to her room and cry, burying her face in the coverlet of her bed where she had thrown herself, no one can say; for nobody ever knew from Elly what torrents of tears came after that thunderstorm, nor how she trembled, and wondered, and doubted if papa were really so noble, so good, so fine a gentleman as she had asserted him to be.

'They will never consent,' said Mrs. Egerton, after the girl had gone, 'Oh, Jack, I wish I could believe as she does, that my brother—— But I will not deceive you, Jack. He will never, never consent. He is a proud man, though she does not know it—there are no such proud people as these simple people. I wish, I wish I could think as she does: but I can't, I can't, Jack!'

'Do you really wish it, Mrs. Egerton,' said John, taking her hand and kissing it. 'I could not have expected that. It is more than I had any right to hope.'

'Did I say I wished it? I can't tell. She and you draw the heart out of my breast. I ought not to wish it. Oh, Jack, my poor Jack, this is a dreadful thing to bear.'

He let her hand go with a deep sigh. 'Who can feel that as I do?' he said.

'You; oh, but it is different with you. The man (I am sure I beg your pardon) is your father. It is your duty to put up with him: it is not for you to bring up his sins against him. But we that have nothing to do with him— Jack, oh, Jack, the cases are different! and you say yourself that Elly ought not—that she knows nothing of the world.'

It was ungenerous to appeal to what he had himself said. But he consented with a melancholy movement of his head.

'The rector has always been very kind to me. Oh, yes, I know that's a different thing altogether. It is not like giving me—— Mrs. Egerton, I think I had better go away, for what is the use of talking. He is my father, it is true. It is my business to put up with it, to bear it—to bear everything that follows from it—but it is hard. You can't say but what it is hard.'

'Oh, Jack, my poor boy! She took his hand in both of hers, and, that not being enough, bent forward and kissed him in the anguish of her sympathy. 'But what can I say to you? I can't deceive you. I know they will never, never consent.'

John went away, not knowing where he went, as if he were following his own funeral. He felt like that, he said to himself, sadly—the funeral of all his hopes. He had his work, but what would that be, what could it matter if he made his fortune, without Elly? And then he went on reflecting, as many a man has done before him, on the spite of fate. If this had all happened before he went to Edgeley, how much less would the misery have been! It would have been bad enough, but he could have thrown it off, and perhaps in time have forgotten it: for then Elly was but a light of his childhood faint and far-off, and had not become a necessity of his life. Why was he permitted to go and see her again, to discover all that she was to him, only to lose her for ever? For Elly had been right in what she had said in her indignation, 'A girl's own mind is nothing.' Even John, though he had perfect trust in her, though for a moment he had been carried away by the flash of her resolution and certainty, did not take much comfort now from Elly's pledge. She did not understand (how should she?) what thing it was that so lightly, so easily, she made up her mind to take upon herself. Poor John put that aside in the deep despondency that overwhelmed him. And, when his mind recurred to his momentary triumph of the morning, it but added a pang the more. To think that this success had secured the only thing that had been needed a little while ago; and, now he had got it, it was nothing. He went slowly, slowly away, following (he said to himself again) his own funeral, not able to hold up his head.

CHAPTER XVIII.

A SUSPENDED SOLUTION.

IT seemed to matter very little to John that Mr. Cattley met him in the evening with what he thought good news. In the absence of anything better, it was good news. May had been very amiable, as was the manner of that hopeless but good-humoured and philosophical unfortunate. He declared that nothing on earth would induce him to injure his children by attaching himself to them: he had come back to John's room only to return those papers which he had taken with the intention of disposing of them on his son's account, meaning no harm. He had never meant any harm. He had intended, perhaps, to secure to himself a share of the profit, but never to harm the boy. 'Though he's sadly changed, if ever he was my little chap,' he said.

Mr. Cattley did not tell Jack, but he confided to Susie that he had offered to take that smiling and gentle-mannered reprobate to live with 'us' in the new parish where nobody would have known. But May would not listen to any such proposal. He was very wise and foreseeing, and full of consideration.

'There is no saying who might turn up,' he said; 'at the last, everything gets known; and perhaps a parson's house would be too much for me,' he had added, with a twinkle in his eyes. 'I don't know that I'm good enough for that. I might fall into temptation, don't you know! And I couldn't live with a blunderbuss always at my head, which would be the case if I were with that son of mine—if he is my son. And Susie would be worse, with her eyes. I remember her eyes long ago—they were harder to meet than all her mother's talk. They're all very good, Mr. Cattley. A man might be very happy among them; but not my kind. I'm not worthy of such company. No, I've got a plan of my own.'

This plan, when it was stated, was to the effect that May had made up his mind to emigrate. He thought he would go to the far West of America, or to California.

'I don't want to go to a place where there's no fun,' he avowed, candidly. 'I want to see a little life. If I stay here, I'll get into mischief.'

Mr. Cattley (against his own wishes) had done his best to persuade him to depart from this determination, but in vain; and finally he had been authorised to treat with the family for the passage-money of the two travellers, for Mr. Cattley had found the faithful Joe in attendance, and had not been able to persuade May that this was not a fit companion for him.

'He has been all the company I've had. Perhaps he's not fit for respectable society,' said May, looking at the slouching ruffian with eyes that were almost affectionate, 'but I'm not respectable myself, and why should I pretend to be better than he is? I'm not better, I'm worse, if the truth was known; for of course I know a great deal better, and ought to have avoided what was wrong, if anything is really wrong or right in this world. It depends so much on your point of view.'

'But why should you not be respectable?' the curate had said. 'There is a home waiting for you, and better company than Joe.'

The unteachable, the never-to-be-convinced, shook his head. 'Joe will suit me best,' he said. And thus the bargain was made. He was to have a moderate allowance, his passage-money, and his outfit. He was shipped off with his friend, decently clothed, well fitted out as he desired, and disappeared into the West. When his children, half-glad, half-miserable, went to see him off, he bade them be cheerful and not fret. 'For there is no telling when the fancy may take me, and I may turn up again,' he said. The hearts of Susie and John sank within them at this last blessing which he flung at them over the side of the ship, which was already beginning to churn the water on her passage outward-bound. They did not see the twinkle in his eye, nor know that he meant it for a joke in the humorous simplicity of his heart.

Susie married her curate shortly after, very quietly, without any fuss, in London, an event which caused much excitement in Edgeley, but none where it took place. The Rev. Percy Spencer never mentioned it at all, or allowed that he knew of it. But he spoke of 'that fool Cattley,' and was so violent about the late curate's mismanagement of the parish that even the mild rector, who never made any appearance save in extremity, took up the cudgels on behalf of the absent.

'It will be well for you if you do half as much for the parish in your day as Cattley did in his,' the rector said; and his son aghast at this unexpected defence ventured to say no more. Mrs. Egerton treated the matter in the contrary way. She made, perhaps, too great a joke of it, talking to everybody on the subject. 'Such a good thing for him,' she said, 'going into a new place: and a good little nonentity of a wife who will adore him, which is what our good Mr. Cattley was little used to.' But she sent the pair a wedding present, and was what Susie called very kind. This marriage was no help to Elly, however, in the arduous piece of work which she found she had before her when she got home. It made matters a little worse. It turned Percy into an open and violent foe, and it shook a little the wavering sympathy which Mrs. Egerton always accorded her. And as for the rector, whom Elly had declared her faith in, he did not respond as she had hoped. He was a true gentleman, he was as good as Chaucer's 'very parfit gentle knight'—he was all his daughter had claimed for him to be. But he, too, shuddered at the name of the convict. Like all the older people, he remembered May's story, and all about him: and to permit his daughter, the quintessence of the family excellence and pride, the flower of all the kindred, to connect herself with such a race was more than Mr. Spencer's generosity, or his kindness, or even Elly's influence could bring him to. He retired into that stronghold of silence which is so redoubtable. He would not argue nor give his reasons; he would not enter into the abstract question. He acknowledged, or at least he did not contest, the merits of John. But, when all was said that Elly's fervid eloquence could say, the rector remained unresponsive and unshaken.

'One might as well try to get an answer out of a stone wall,' Elly cried, in hot exasperation to her aunt.

'Oh, my dear, didn't I tell you so? I told poor Jack so and he believed me, but you would not believe me. He will never, never consent.'

'Then he shall never, never be asked any more!' cried Elly, in her indignation.

But this was a thing which it was not practicable to carry out. He was asked again and again, and continued to be asked until the time when Elly should come of age, and then she was determined to take her own way.

'I am disappointed in papa,' she wrote to John, 'but it is not out of his heart he does it. He has not a word to say for himself. When I have showed him the question in a just light, and proved that all their objections are prejudice and nonsense, he just goes back to where he was at first and shakes his head. But never mind. In two years' (in a year and a half—in a year—according as time went on, for this formula was repeated on several occasions) 'I shall be of age. You cannot say that I don't know the world or that I am too young *then*; and they all know what I am going to do.'

John could not refuse to take comfort from this repeated and unwavering pledge. He had plunged into the preliminaries of his work without a moment's delay, and very soon, at an age when in England most young men are only beginning to wonder what they shall do, he found himself at the head of one of the greatest undertakings in the country, the centre of endless activity. Such advancement perhaps, everything favouring, comes sooner in his profession than in any other. But nobody, except those who had seen him grow up, suspected how young Mr. Sandford really was, and even those who did know it could scarcely believe in the accuracy of their own memory. He had always been older than his years, and the great shock he had received in the discovery of his father threw him so far apart from all the thoughts and occupations of youth, that it seems to John himself like half-a-century, that age of doubt and of misery, when everything was at its lowest ebb, before the upspringing of new hope. That grave youth matured under the fire of suffering into something like a precocious middle-age, or at least the steadiest, sternest manhood. He grew to be both respected and feared before he was five-and-twenty. And, what was curious, the resemblance to his father, which had been chiefly, perhaps, in the imagination of the elders, died completely away. He became like Mrs. Sandford in these days of strong activity and doubtful hope: not severe to his men, the multitude of work-people of all classes who now laboured under him, a whole little world of clerks, engineers, artisans, and labourers in every grade. He was not severe ever: it was said indeed that he took circumstances into consideration and tempered justice with mercy when any fault was pointed out at the office or among the men, far more than most masters do, and was slow to lose patience with any young culprit; but he looked severe, which is the same thing—nay, is better as a deterrent. The people under him were afraid of the stern look of his youthful unimpeachable virtue: whereas, if he had been as severe in fact as in looks, a natural antagonism, the protest of nature against harshness, would have speedily evolved itself.

There are some things, however, which John has not been able to do, notwithstanding his great success. He has never been able to move his mother from the position in which she has so firmly placed herself. Mrs. Sandford spoke no more of her husband than was inevitable; she never recurred to the subject with John, never mentioned it to Susie except on that one morning when Mr. Cattley was first introduced to her: but she took upon herself all the arrangements that were made by Mr. Cattley for May's comfort, not permitting either son or daughter to interfere. Susie was proud of this fact, while John with a grudge understood it at least—that the proud woman could speak more freely to a stranger than to her children, of the man who had been the ruin of her own life. She would not see her husband, however, and never spoke of him, nor gave the least indication of any knowledge on the subject. If she was aware of the time of his departure, she made no sign of knowing it. There was no relenting in her, no affection, only a horror beyond words. And she would not allow John, when he began to grow rich, to remove her from the laborious post which it seemed no longer right that the mother of a rising man, with plenty of money at his disposal, should continue to hold. She smiled at the suggestion, and dismissed it with a wave of her hand. To return to the little house at Edgeley among all the village people, which was what John in youthful ignorance, notwithstanding his precocious middle-age, would have liked her to do, was indeed impossible. What would she have done there? unless, indeed, the cholera had broken out, or some tremendous epidemic, when she could have organised hospitals. John, however, here let us allow, with a great want of perception, was annoyed that she should not have accepted this proposal of his, and retired and given herself repose after her hard-working life. But Mrs. Sandford was not one of the people who long for rest. 'The wages of going on' was what pleased her most, and work, and her own way. John was not pleased; it would have soothed him to think that his mother was resting and doing nothing in that little house, which he kept up always with an obstinate determination that it should be, if not a grateful retirement for anyone, at least the shrine of departed innocence and peace.

We will not conceal from the reader that Elly is now twenty-one and more, but that the marriage has not yet taken place. There has been sickness and trouble at Edgeley, and the only daughter of the house has not been able to withdraw from the post of duty: but since she became of age she and her betrothed have corresponded fully. She knows everything that goes on at the works, and all the new steps John is taking, and received telegrams three or four times a day when that dreadful catastrophe occurred which everyone has read of, when the machinery broke down and the water poured back into the old channels, and for a moment everything seemed in jeopardy. John dragged her into that as if she had been his head clerk: he demanded her sympathy at every moment, clamouring in her ears with his telegrams, in a way which excited all the village. Indeed, there has been no political convulsion, no contested election, no crime or accident for fifty years, which has thrilled through Edgeley like that supposed collapse of the works in the Thames Valley. When all was right, the whole community began to breathe again. Dick, who was at home on furlough, trudged backward and forward between the rectory and the post-office for several days, too impatient to wait for the telegraph boy: and when it was all over he was the man who electrified the rectory and all the community by saying, 'This will never do.' Dick was a man of few words, like his father; an easy-going man who let other people manage most of his affairs for him; but when much enforced he would say a word of weight all the more startling from its rarity. He said these words one evening after dinner in the midst of the family, suddenly when nobody expected it. He brought down his hand upon the table, not roughly, but with sufficient sound to call attention, and he said,

'This will never do. This business about Elly and Jack. He is a better man than any of us. What does it matter who was his father? He's his own father, and all his relations. And that Mrs. Cattley's a sweet little woman. Don't let's have any more nonsense about it,' said Dick.

The rector gasped, and Mrs. Egerton fell a-crying, and Percy rose and left the table. But Elly held out her hand to her big brother, and the thing was as good as settled from that day.

Let it be a comfort to all virtuous young persons in a similar position that, as long as they hold out and are firm and constant, some one will always arise at the end and face all obstructions with the verdict of good sense and honest sympathy, saying in face of all unnecessary objections, whether of birth or of money: 'This will never do.'

But with all his success, and with the happiness which is about to come, one great cloud remains on John Sandford's life, a fear which sometimes takes his breath away and makes his heart sick, the fear that some day when he suspects nothing, some sweet day—it might be his marriage morning, it might be any happy anniversary—there will suddenly appear round a corner a stumbling, shambling figure, never without a certain attractiveness even in its degradation, a sort of charm of careless innocence in the midst of guilt. Sometimes when he goes through the works with perhaps a little elation in the greatness of his undertaking and the consciousness of the crowd which looks up to him as master, surrounding him with that veiled obsequiousness which makes the head of great industrial enterprises like a little king—the sight of some shadow in the distance will take all the strength and courage out of him.

'There is no telling when the fancy may take me.' These words come back to his ears with a meaning far more than was ever intended. But as a matter of fact there is cause enough to fear. For May never meant anything steadily or for long all his life. And when the fun to which he looked forward is exhausted—which is a thing that soon happens on the shady side of life—who can tell that the fancy may not take him to bring the remnants of his worn-out existence home? Poor wretch, for whom love and honour do not exist, but only fear and pity! the good man, the prosperous and happy, who has deserved his prosperity, as well as the other deserved his misery, is still the Son of His Father, and still bound for ever in this world at least, wretchedness to well-being, honour to shame.

There is, however, one way in which this piece of personal history may be safely made to end like a fairy-tale. Susie and her curate went home to their new parish like a pair of doves to their nest. And these two lived happy ever after, if ever any pair did so in this troubled yet not always miserable world.

THE END.

Milton Keynes UK
Ingram Content Group UK Ltd.
UKHW020831200524
442968UK00005B/572